ANOTHER WORLD

11

WHISPERS FROM THE PAST

Soaps™
& Serials

PIONEER COMMUNICATIONS NETWORK, INC.

Whispers from the Past

ANOTHER WORLD paperback novels are published and distributed by Pioneer Communications Network, Inc.

SOAPS & SERIALS™ is a trademark of Pioneer Communications Network, Inc.

ISBN: 1-55726-050-8

Printed in Canada

10 9 8 7 6 5 4 3 2 1

ALICE FRAME knew the time had come to assume her role as president of Frame Enterprises. It was what her late husband would have wanted. But she wasn't prepared for the game of dirty pool she'd be forced to play with Steve's brother, Willis.

SHARLENE WATTS was on to the scheming power play Willis was making for control of Frame Enterprises. But Willis's threats to tell her fiancé the terrible truth of her past were enough to keep her silent—and terrified.

MARIANNE RANDOLPH felt responsible for her parents' separation. But her attempts to reunite them backfired when she learned the truth about her father's infidelities. Betrayed and confused, she wondered if she'd ever trust again.

Series Story Editor **Mary Ann Cooper** is America's foremost soap opera expert. She writes the nationally syndicated column *Speaking of Soaps*, is a major contributor to soap opera magazines, and has appeared on numerous radio and television talk shows.

Author **Chloe Seid** has written various books, magazine articles, and television shows. For eleven years she worked as a consultant to one of the major broadcasting networks in New York City. During that time Chloe was involved with several Emmy award winning television productions.

From the editor's desk...

Dear Friend,

Captivating . . . exciting . . . heartwarming . . . these are but a few of the comments we've received from Soaps & Serials readers. We're delighted. Every month the fine team of writers and editors at Pioneer pool all their resources to bring you seven new spectacular books.

Based on actual scripts from ANOTHER WORLD, each novel is written with you in mind. Soaps & Serials take you back to the very beginning of the show, revealing the innocent and infamous pasts of your favorite characters, recreating cherished moments from your favorite episodes. And though each book is a complete, satisfying read, our sensational cliffhanger ending is just a hint of the drama that will unfold in next month's Soaps & Serials book.

We've recently received numerous requests for previous volumes of Soaps & Serials. If you are also curious about how it all began—or if you want to complete your collection—please see the order form inserted in this book.

For Soaps & Serials,

Rosalind Noonan

Rosalind Noonan
Editor-in-Chief
Pioneer Communications Network, Inc.

Mary Ann Remembers

ANOTHER WORLD

Everybody knows that one of the ingredients of a successful soap is a hateful villain or villainess. I remember when Robin Strasser first created the role of Rachel Davis on ANOTHER WORLD. I couldn't stand her, and neither could my friends. Rachel was manipulative and cruel. How she tormented Alice Matthews and Steven Frame!

When Victoria Wyndham took over the part, I began to notice that Rachel was beginning to show signs of a heart. Harding Lemay, the head writer for ANOTHER WORLD, clearly loved the character. At first, Rachel's happy marriage to business tycoon Mac Cory created an undercurrent of resentment among the viewers. She didn't deserve such happiness. Producers recognized that viewers would only feel right about liking Rachel if the character went through a baptism of fire—a catharsis—to wipe out her evil past. Thus, she suffered at the hands of Iris Carrington, Mac's spoiled daughter. As she went through the ordeal, fans wrote in by the thousands to voice their concern and affection. Rachel emerged from this crisis to become one of the most beloved characters on ANOTHER WORLD.

Chapter One
Trouble

"How could you, Iris?" Mac Cory cried as he stormed through the door into his daughter's elegant living room. "How could you do something so cruel?"

Iris Delaney cringed. She had never seen her beloved father so angry. He must have found out, she thought wildly. Still, she made sure to look innocent. "Daddy, please calm down," she soothed. "I don't know what you're talking about. I haven't done anything."

Mac faced her, his eyes blazing. "Oh, really? From what I've heard, you're responsible for Rachel's miscarriage. For the loss of our child," he thundered.

So, despite her efforts to hide it, the truth was finally coming out. She forced herself to think calmly; there had to be a way she could turn this around, she reasoned. After all, if there was anything she was good at, it was lying her way out of a jam. *Damn Rachel*, she thought irritably. Nothing had been the same between her and her father since Rachel had come into his life.

What Mac saw in his wife was a mystery to Iris. Certainly she was pretty enough, with her dark hair and heart-shaped face, but as far as Iris was concerned, Rachel was just a social climber from the wrong side of the tracks. And keeping undeserving women like Rachel away from her publishing-magnate father was second nature to Iris—especially women who were younger than she was. But now it was obvious from the fury on Mac's face that she had gone too far. She was more afraid than she had ever been in her life.

"I don't know why you're saying such awful things to me, Daddy," she cooed, trying to hide her fear. "I wouldn't hurt you. I love you."

"So you've always said." Mac faced his daughter. She looked so tiny and vulnerable that he almost weakened. Then he remembered all the pain she had caused, and his resolve returned. "And what about Rachel? I suppose you're going to tell me you've always loved her, too?" he asked bitterly.

Iris knew she had to answer cautiously. "Well, no, I've never thought Rachel was quite right for you. But I have been trying my best to get along with her since your marriage."

Mac looked incredulous. "Oh, really?"

"It's true. I offered to build that studio on your estate so Rachel would have a place to do her sculpture, didn't I?"

"A bribe," he replied bluntly. "I thought it was a nice gesture at the time, but now I'm convinced you only did it to confuse Rachel about your true motives."

Calculated tears sprang into Iris's eyes. She knew from years of experience that her father couldn't stand to see her cry. "That's so unfair. All I ever wanted was for you to be happy."

Mac grabbed his daughter's shoulders and shook her. "How dare you lie to me! My happiness is the last thing you care about," he said angrily. "All you want," he cried, spitting out the words, "is to manipulate me for your own selfish reasons. And I must say you've done an excellent job of it!"

Now Iris was crying in earnest. "I don't know what you're talking about," she sobbed, flinging herself down on the peach-silk divan.

Mac ran a hand through his thick gray hair and tried to gain control of his anger. "Then I will explain it to you. Now sit up and listen to me."

Wiping her eyes with a lace handkerchief she'd found in her dressing gown pocket, Iris did as she was told.

"On the night Rachel miscarried, I was here having drinks with you and Robert. You remember that, don't you?"

Iris nodded. She remembered all too clearly. She'd been annoyed that evening because her father wasn't paying any attention to her friend Tracey DeWitt, who was also one of his former girlfriends. He had come over to have cocktails with Iris and her architect husband, Robert Delaney, and to see Tracey's photographs for a book she was preparing.

"When Rachel began feeling sick, she called here—" Mac continued.

Iris interrupted. "Several people called that night."

"She called here," he repeated, glaring at his daughter, "and she asked to speak to me. But you told her that I was too busy to come to the phone. And later, when I tried to phone her to say I'd be late, the line was busy. Naturally, I assumed she was talking to Ada. When I got home, I found her on the floor with the telephone in her hand. Now I learn she collapsed just after talking to you."

"Did Rachel tell you that?" Iris asked, suddenly confident again. "You know how confused she was, what with the hemorrhaging and then losing the baby during surgery."

"Confused? That's just what you wanted her to think. During those hours after she miscarried, Rachel drifted in and out of consciousness, and the whole time she kept calling out to me. 'Mac, why didn't you come?' she'd ask. Can you imagine how guilty I felt?"

Iris could imagine. She had felt a little guilty —and very scared—herself. That was why she had rushed to Bay City General to see Rachel, tired and groggy though she was. She had convinced Rachel that she'd only dreamed she'd called Iris's house trying to reach Mac. Where had Rachel learned the truth? Iris wondered. Moreover, was it too late to do something about it?

"That was one of the worst nights of my life," Mac said, looking Iris directly in the eye. "Dr. Gilchrist said Rachel was delirious from her fever, but now I find out she knew exactly what she was saying."

She pounced on this statement. "But don't you see? Dr. Gilchrist knows people say all kinds of things when they're ill. Of course Rachel wished you were home, but that doesn't mean she actually called you here."

Mac ignored her comments and went on, his voice thick with emotion. "And then, after her surgery. . . . Do you remember what Rachel said then, Iris? She said, 'Put Mac on the phone, Iris. Tell him I need him.' I asked you about those words, and you lied to my face. 'Rachel's just confused,' you assured me. And like a fool, I believed you. Your own mother died in childbirth!" he reminded her, his voice shaking with outrage. "How could you permit even the possibility of that happening to someone else?" His face twisted with anger. "What kind of a person are you?"

"Daddy," Iris cried, sobbing anew, "I don't know who made up these horrible lies, but someone is saying all this just to tear us apart. If it's Rachel, well, I'm sure she's just doing this to hurt us."

"Yes, Rachel told me. I practically had to force it out of her. However, if you don't think I should believe Rachel, I can call a person who knows the whole story."

"Who?" Iris asked, dreading the answer.

"Tracey DeWitt."

She shuddered. Tracey was an old friend Iris had brought to town to break up Mac and Rachel's marriage. Unfortunately, Tracey had disliked her shabby treatment of Mac and his wife so much, she'd left Bay City. But Iris had assumed they were still friends and was now disturbed to think Tracey may have betrayed that friendship.

"So," Mac asked, moving toward the phone, "shall we call Tracey?"

Iris sprang to her feet. "No, don't."

His eyes narrowed. "Then you admit that you were the cause of this tragedy."

"No, of course I wasn't," she denied. "But there's no point in calling Tracey. She'd only lie about the whole thing."

"Why would she do that?"

"Tracey has never forgiven me for breaking up your relationship with her. I'm sure she's making up these stories just to even the score."

"Everyone's lying but you, is that it?" Mac questioned archly.

She tilted her blond head and looked at her father with her most vulnerable expression. "Please believe me," she implored.

He stared at her in disbelief. "It won't work. For too long you've been able to look at me with those big, wide eyes and I would melt. I suppose it's my fault," he added, reflectively. "I felt so guilty that I didn't have more time for you when you were growing up that I stupidly tried to make it up to you by giving in to your every whim."

"Don't say that," she cried. "You've been a wonderful father."

"No, I haven't. Because of me, you've turned into a selfish, spoiled woman who would put someone else's life in danger just to get her own way."

The calm her father was exhibiting frightened Iris even more than his anger. "What are you going to do?" she whispered at last.

"Do?" Mac looked at her with contempt. "I'm going home to my wife, and I'm going to pray that she and I can have another child together. Because as of this moment, I have no children."

"What?"

"You heard me," Mac said quietly, heading toward the door. "I don't ever want to hear from you again, and I don't want to hear about you. Starting now, you are out of my life." He let himself out of her apartment and did not look back.

For one long moment, Iris stared at the door in disbelief. Then she broke into fresh sobs as she ran into her bedroom. Throwing herself down onto the luxurious bed, she cried as if her heart were breaking. The only man she had ever truly loved was abandoning her.

I hate Rachel, she thought, pounding her small fists hard against the bed. Couldn't Mac see that she was just trying to free him from Rachel's clutches? Everyone in town knew Rachel was a troublemaker. She had practically ruined Alice Matthews's life by trying to steal Steve Frame away from her. Rachel had even gotten pregnant with Steve's child, and then tried to pass him off as the son of Russ Matthews, the man she'd been married to at the time. What could be lower than that? Iris wondered. People may have been saying that Rachel had changed since her marriage to Mac, but Iris didn't believe it for a second.

But although Iris was certain that Rachel was all

wrong for her father, it had never occurred to her that some of the less desirable qualities she associated with her father's wife—such as scheming to get her own way—were traits she herself displayed. Quite recently, for instance, she had duped an unsuspecting Robert Delaney into marrying her, just the way Rachel had tricked both Russ and Steve into wedlock.

The bright sun filtered into Iris's bedroom, and although her heart was heavy, her crying slowly stopped. There had to be a way she could change her father's mind, there just had to. But even with her fertile imagination, she couldn't quite come up with anything.

Snapshots from the past filled her mind: of Mac buying her a pony when she was six; of her crying because she had to leave her motherless home and go off to a Swiss boarding school at age ten; the gold-framed picture of her father she'd taken wherever she went; of her walking proudly on his arm when she made her debut. She had to get him back, no matter what it took.

Slowly, Iris's thoughts strayed to another man —her husband. Perhaps Robert could help her patch things up with Mac.

Daddy likes Robert, she thought happily. *Robert will be able to fix it. I know he will.* She repeated the words over and over in her head like a magic charm until she fell into a troubled sleep.

Robert Delaney felt the wind whipping off the bay and pulled his scarf a bit more tightly around his neck. Even though it was finally spring, the warm weather still had not arrived. A fat robin sat on the sparse park lawn, looking up at him as if to say, "I'm here, so it really must be spring." But Robert didn't buy it; he wouldn't until he could put his heavy coat away for good.

He had taken the long route from his office to the Frame Enterprises building, hoping to clear his head. His personal problems were taking up too much of his energy these days, and he was finding it difficult to concentrate on business. But he didn't want to think about Iris any longer, so as he walked into the steel and glass edifice that housed Frame Enterprises, he tried to turn his attention to the business at hand. But as he rode the elevator up to the construction division, Robert realized he wished he was anywhere but there.

When Steve Frame was alive, Robert had enjoyed his work as architect for the company's many projects. But the joy had gone out of it since his friend's untimely death. Still, he felt an obligation to Steve's widow, Alice, to be on call if she needed him. He also genuinely liked Vic Hastings, Steve's second-in-command, who was now running Frame Construction, by far the company's largest department. Vic was a smart, caring supervisor. Things were going so well, in fact, an in-house architect, Carol Lamonte, had been added to the staff.

Carol's presence might have bothered Robert, both personally and professionally, as he had once had an affair with Carol that hadn't ended very well. All that seemed to be behind them, however, and he and Carol were able to treat each other simply as colleagues. As for the work, Robert's architectural firm was so busy with its own projects, he was glad the responsibilities for Frame Construction were no longer entirely on his shoulders. But one thing about the changes at Frame did bother Robert terribly: Willis Frame's attitude.

Shortly before Steve's death, his younger brother, Willis, had come to Bay City. Steve had gladly given him a position at the construction company, and Willis seemed to be doing a good job. What annoyed Robert was his proprietary air about company affairs. He sometimes acted as if he, not Vic, ran Frame Construction. Robert was relieved that today he would just be meeting with Carol.

Still, the meeting might turn out to be tense, regardless. Vic seemed to think that there were some problems with the huge shopping center project Carol was working on. *He* hadn't been able to get much out of her but thought that Carol might talk to Robert, architect to architect. If there were difficulties, Robert could then offer her some professional advice. He sighed as he got off the elevator and walked into the Frame offices. He just hoped he was enough of a diplomat to carry the whole thing off.

"Hi there, Robert," Sharlene Watts said. "You don't look very happy to see us this morning."

Robert smiled down at Sharlene, who was sitting at the reception desk. "Not true. I'm always happy to see you." Sharlene was Steven and Willis's sister and had been pitching in at the construction company. She was staying with Alice temporarily, and it was through her that Sharlene had met Alice's brother, Dr. Russ Matthews. From what

Robert understood, they were dating pretty seriously.

Sharlene checked the appointment book and then looked back at him. "Well, according to this, you're here to see Carol."

"That's right, he is." Robert turned around and saw that Carol had come out to the front desk to greet him. Even after all the time that had passed, his heart jumped a little when he saw her willowly blond loveliness. But he put those feelings firmly aside and put on a professional face.

"How are you?" he asked, smiling.

"Fine. Shall we go into my office?"

Robert nodded his assent and followed Carol into a well-lit room off the main corridor. Plans were neatly laid out on her drafting table, and the lush plants on the windowsill added a homey touch that contrasted with the distant, formal look that pervaded the outer offices of Frame Construction. She pulled up a chair for him and then sat down at her desk.

"Would you like some coffee?" Carol offered. "I can ask Sharlene to bring some in."

"Please don't bother. I feel like I've been drinking coffee all day."

"I know how that is," she answered politely. It was obvious that Carol was waiting for him to state his business now that the pleasantries were over. Robert decided there was nothing to do but plunge in.

"How's the shopping center project going? I hear it's going to be quite a structure."

"It's moving right along," she answered brightly.

"Most of the outside work has been done and the electricians are starting to lay the wires."

"No problems?" Robert probed.

Carol toyed with a pencil. Her delicate features seemed incongruously feminine behind the heavy wooden desk. Finally, she shrugged. "There are always problems on big jobs like this. You know that."

Robert let out a small chuckle. "That's for sure. Either the deliveries are screwed up, or there are union troubles . . ."

"We've had our share of both, but everything is under control now," she said, looking him right in the eye.

"That's good," he replied, slightly embarrassed that she seemed to have seen through him so clearly. "This project is really your baby, huh?"

"Mine and Willis's," she confirmed. "He was the one who went out and put the deal together."

"I thought making deals was Vic's job."

"It usually is," she said, leaning back in her chair, "but Willis was the one who had all the contacts on this one. He really did a marvelous job."

There was a knock on the slightly opened door, and then Willis stuck his head inside the room. "Did I just hear my name and the word 'marvelous' in the same sentence?"

"Hi, there," Carol said, her eyes lighting up. "I thought you were going to be out of town today."

"I handled the whole thing by phone. Hello,

Robert," he said, coming over to shake the other man's hand. "To what do we owe the pleasure?"

"Nothing special. I just dropped in for a little shop talk with Carol."

"She's doing a great job for Frame Construction," Willis said, bestowing a happy smile on Carol.

"That's what I like to hear," Robert said, "praise for the architect."

"I sure can pick them, can't I?" Willis asked.

Robert wasn't sure if he meant personally or professionally. "You two are quite a mutual admiration society," he said, laughing lightly and getting to his feet.

"Are you leaving already?" Carol asked, rising to see him out. In spite of her words, she certainly did not seem in a hurry to have him stay.

"I'm afraid I have to. I'm expected at a meeting at my office in a little while."

"Well, I'm glad you stopped by," she said graciously. "When you're here on business, it seems as though we never have time to really talk."

"Maybe we could have lunch together some time," Robert suggested.

"I'd like that," Carol replied.

Robert and Willis then said their good-byes. The moment Robert was out the door, Willis turned to question Carol. "What did he want?"

She shrugged. "Not much. I think he still feels responsible for our architectural work."

"Well, we don't need him," Willis snapped.

"Willis, Robert still does most of Frame's big jobs. I don't think it's so strange he'd want to come over and talk once in a while."

He looked at her sullenly. "I see Vic Hastings's hand in all this."

"Vic? What do you mean?"

"He probably sent Robert over here to check up on the shopping center project."

"He did bring it up," Carol admitted.

"Did he know there were problems?" Willis asked, his voice urgent.

"I'm not sure. He didn't seem to know anything specific, I could tell that much."

Willis looked at her intently. "And you didn't tell him anything?" Carol shook her head. "Nothing slipped?" he pressed.

"Of course not," she assured him.

"But you did get the impression he was here to talk about the shopping center?"

Carol considered the question. "We really didn't talk about anything else."

He turned away from her, the pieces now coming together. "Vic must suspect that there are going to be cost overruns on this project. If he finds out for sure, we're in trouble."

"The overruns may not be too bad."

"They'd better not be," he snapped. "The last thing I need is Hastings on my case."

Carol walked over to Willis and slipped her arms around his neck. "Don't worry about it."

His expression softened a little. "If I'm not worrying, my mind has to be on something else," he teased.

"I think I can arrange that," she said in a husky voice.

"Oh, yeah? Let's see."

She pulled him closer and touched her lips to his. Then she ran a hand through his hair and kissed him more passionately. Willis responded to her caresses, but Carol didn't succeed in taking his mind off his problems.

Even as Carol kissed him, Willis continued thinking about Robert's visit and Vic's part in it. *Forget it, Vic*, he thought. *This is Frame Construction, and there's only one person who's going to run it—Willis Frame.*

Chapter Two
Parents and Children

Pat Randolph was curled up on her couch, staring out the picture window. Raindrops were streaming down the pane, interrupted only by an occasional leaf whipped against the glass by the wind.

Pat's patrician features were locked in an expression of profound sadness. She didn't know how long she had been sitting there, nor did she care. Every once in a while, her gaze strayed to the locked liquor cabinet. It was an agonizing temptation, but Pat refused to give in to it. Liquor had caused nothing but trouble in her life and things were difficult enough now without adding that complication.

Turning her head slightly, Pat was able to see the framed photographs that adorned the mantel. She sighed as she looked at them. Caught by the camera at joyful moments, her family smiled back at her. *Too bad things have to change,* she thought.

She glanced at the picture of her parents on their thirtieth anniversary, gaily toasting each other with champagne. Her mother, Mary, was gone now. A photograph of herself, taken years ago with her siblings, Russ and Alice, brought a tiny smile to her face. They were so carefree back then, not even suspecting some of the ordeals they would have to endure in the future.

Pat's gaze came to rest on the picture of her husband and children. John looked every inch the handsome, attentive father: tall, solid, the kind of man who would always be there for his wife. Only sometimes, he wasn't. Laughing up at John in the picture were their twins, Michael and Marianne. How happy they looked. The picture had been taken as a surprise for Pat's birthday, and she could see the fun and mischief in their faces. Of course, that picture had been taken quite a while ago, when all the Randolphs had adored each other. Now the family was deeply divided, and Pat wasn't sure that would ever change.

"Mom, what are you doing sitting there in the dark?" Marianne asked sharply, switching on a light.

Pat blinked and looked at the tawny-haired young woman who so resembled herself at nineteen. "Oh, Marianne. I didn't hear you come in."

"What were you doing?" she persisted.

"Not much," Pat answered with a short laugh. She stretched, then settled back against the couch. "Thinking, I suppose."

"About Dr. Gilchrist?" Marianne asked sharply.

"I've told you about a hundred times that Dave is

just a friend. He was a friend of yours at one time, too," Pat pointed out.

"He was my doctor," Marianne corrected as she sat down stiffly in a high-backed wing chair. "So, what were you thinking about?" she questioned, changing the subject.

"Among other things, I was considering getting a job."

"A job?" Marianne repeated, startled.

"Don't you think I'm capable of holding a job?" Pat asked, rather amused.

"It's not that," Marianne protested. "It's just . . . what do you need a job for? Daddy gives you plenty of money."

Pat stood up and restlessly paced the floor. "Your father may not always give me money. Besides, I need something to do with my time. Surely, you can understand that."

"Well, why don't you go to work in Daddy's law office. He always needs someone there to help with the filing and things."

Daddy, Daddy, Daddy. Pat thought she was going to scream, but she managed to control herself. "Honey, you know your father and I have been separated for weeks. There's a very good chance that we"—she stumbled a little over the next words—"that we won't stay married at all. Considering the circumstances, I could hardly start working in your father's office now."

With a furious look on her face, Marianne stormed out of the room and into the kitchen. She began flinging cupboard doors open. Her mother was right behind her. "Do you want me to fix you something?" she asked.

"I can fix my own dinner," Marianne shot back as she opened a can of soup. "So why this sudden rush to start talking about divorce? Are you afraid Dr. Gilchrist won't wait around for you?"

"I'm not even going to dignify that with an answer," Pat said, raising her voice. "I told you not two minutes ago how I feel about Dave."

Marianne turned and faced her mother. "Then tell me, why are you in such a hurry to divorce Daddy?"

Pat's heart sank. This was just the kind of discussion she'd wanted to avoid. It would break Marianne's heart if she found out the truth about her father. "I didn't say anything was going to happen right away. I just said I'm sure we're both thinking about going our separate ways."

Marianne poured her soup into a pot. Taking it over to the stove, she began stirring it with a vengeance. "Divorce is the last thing on Daddy's mind. I can tell he wants to get back together with you. If you weren't so stubborn, you'd see it, too. Then we could all be a family again."

It was on the tip of Pat's tongue. With just a little more provocation, she would have told Marianne the whole thing. She would have let it slip that John had been having an affair with his colleague, Barbara Weaver, and that he'd lied to both Pat and Barbara, playing them against each other. Barbara had left John when she'd discovered the truth, and Pat couldn't bring herself to take him back.

Despite her anger, however, Pat didn't think this was the kind of thing Marianne should find out about her father. It was better for her fragile daughter to think that there were just differences between her parents. If she had to play the heavy to save Marianne's feelings, so be it. "Darling, I know you'd like your father and me to reconcile, but sometimes things don't work out the way we want them to."

Marianne barely looked up from the stove. "That's easy to say, but you don't even want to try to make it work. This is all your fault. I hate you."

Suddenly the anger that had been welling up inside Pat spilled out. "Really? I admit I've made my share of mistakes, but I think you have to take a share of the blame."

Marianne's head snapped up as though her mother had slapped her. "Me?"

"Yes, you. Think back for a moment to when this whole mess started. Everything was fine until you got pregnant and then didn't want your father to know about your situation. I couldn't stop you from getting the abortion, although I tried, but I did keep your secret."

"Why do we have to talk about this again?" Marianne muttered. She poured the slightly scorched soup into a bowl and took it to the kitchen table. Pat sat down across from her.

"Because your father was furious with me when he found out that I kept a thing like that from him, that I confided in Dave instead of him."

"You only did what I asked you to," Marianne said wearily. "Daddy should have understood."

"He didn't see it like that, and frankly, I don't blame him. It was the kind of problem a father has every right to know about, and we were very wrong not to tell him."

"If only Aunt Liz hadn't opened her big mouth," Marianne commented, trying to shift the blame at least slightly.

Pat touched her daughter's hand. "It's no good blaming Aunt Liz, honey. Of course she shouldn't have said anything to your father, especially since she found everything out by eavesdropping on your conversation. But we can't change any of that. We just have to move on with our lives."

"That's just it," Marianne countered, suddenly hopeful. "You seem to think that everything has to be different now, but it doesn't. You don't have to move on. You can just go back to the way things were . . . you know, forgive and forget."

Pat rubbed her forehead. How could she forgive John's affair with Barbara? she wondered. How could she forget that Barbara wasn't the first? And perhaps more troubling than anything else, how could she make Marianne understand all this without telling her what kind of a man her father really was?

"So, what do you think, Mom? I could talk to Dad, have him call you?"

"I . . . I don't know."

Marianne dropped her spoon on the table with a clatter. "If you don't want to get back with Dad, there must be a reason. I don't care what you say about Dr.—" The shrill ring of the telephone interrupted her tirade. "I'll get it," she said, getting up and going to the wall phone. "Hello," she answered curtly. "Certainly, she's here." Marianne gave her mother a cynical smile and held out the phone to her. "It's your good friend, Dave Gilchrist," she said sarcastically. She handed the phone to Pat and, without another word, turned and walked out of the room.

Pat watched her leave and sighed. "Hello, Dave," she finally said. "No, nothing's wrong." But she kept her eyes on her daughter until Marianne had disappeared up the stairs.

Alice watched with pride as her adopted daughter, Sally, finished the piece she was playing on the piano. If only Steven were here to see this, she thought, as she had so often recently. She and Steve had been in the process of adopting Sally when his helicopter went down in Australia.

Her gaze wandered around the beautifully appointed living room. All glass and wood, the house had been designed by Steve especially for her, and it was filled with memories. He had been such an integral part of her life, at times it was impossible to believe he was gone. She still half-expected to see him walk through the door.

Their history together was a stormy series of breakups and reunions, but in the end their deep, enduring love for each other had won out. Alice doubted she'd ever find love like that again. One doesn't replace a man like Steve Frame easily.

Just then, Sally came running over and threw herself into Alice's arms. "How was it, Mom?" she asked, flashing her a proud grin.

"Great," Alice said, giving her a kiss. "Just great. You're an absolute prodigy."

"What's that?" Sally asked, wrinkling her nose.

"Someone who can play 'Jingle Bells' after only two lessons." Alice ruffled her daughter's hair.

"Oh, like me?"

"Like you," Alice agreed, wondering if she would ever get enough of this sweet happy child. She was so different now from the sad little girl Alice had first met.

After Steve's accident, friends had suggested that perhaps she shouldn't go through with the adoption, that a small child would be too much for her to handle alone. Alice wouldn't hear of changing her plans, however, needing Sally as much as the young girl needed her.

"Mommy, can I go play in the treehouse?" Sally asked, interrupting Alice's thoughts. Steve had built an elaborate treehouse for his son, Jamie, when the boy was small, and it had become one of Sally's favorite places on the large, wooded estate.

Alice peered out the window. "I don't know, sweetie," she said, looking doubtful. "It's stopped raining, but it's pretty wet out there and its going to be dark soon."

"Please," the child begged. "Just for a little while."

"Alice said no, and I think you should listen to her," Beatrice Gordon said as she came into the room. She hated it when Sally called Alice "Mommy." Beatrice's own daughter, Jenny, was Sally's real mother, and even though she was dead, Beatrice didn't like Alice usurping her title.

It was only coincidence that Beatrice had been working in Bay City as the Corys' housekeeper when the auto accident that took Sally's parents' lives occurred. Beatrice had had a falling out with Jenny years earlier and hadn't even known where she lived. She also had no idea she even had a little granddaughter.

When Beatrice learned the truth about Sally's identity, she decided she wanted to raise her granddaughter herself. If anyone should have custody of Sally, it was Beatrice, she'd reasoned. Finally, however, Beatrice had been convinced that Sally was happy with Alice and should stay there. Beatrice dropped her suit, and Alice asked the older woman to move into the Frame house. She accepted, and now Beatrice ran the household for Alice.

The two women got along fairly well considering the circumstances. Still, some of Alice's child-rearing techniques didn't sit too well with Beatrice and it was all she could do to keep from telling her what she was doing wrong. Some day Alice was going to go too far with her permissiveness, and Beatrice just knew she was going to have to speak her mind.

Alice turned a sunny smile in Beatrice's direction. "If Sally wants to go out for a bit, I think we should let her." She turned to Sally. "But not for very long, maybe fifteen minutes."

Beatrice pursed her lips into a tight, straight line to show her disapproval. Reversing yourself was no way to act with a child, and she wouldn't pretend that she agreed.

"Thanks, Mom," Sally cried.

"You're welcome," Alice replied, her voice light with laughter. "Just bundle up, okay? I'll call you in fifteen minutes."

"I promise," Sally said, bounding out of the room.

"We have a wonderful little girl." Alice smiled wistfully.

"Yes, she is," Beatrice answered, softening. "Would you like your tea now, Alice. I've already put the water on to boil."

Afternoon tea was a habit Alice had picked up when she lived in Europe, and Beatrice usually brought her a cup as well as a light snack in the late afternoon.

"That would be lovely."

"Could I get in on that, too?"

Alice turned around, surprised. "Sharlene, what are you doing home so early?"

Sharlene walked over to the fireplace and rubbed her hands together over the hearth. The warmth of the fire took the chill out of the nippy spring air. "I had a late dentist appointment, so I came home straight from there."

"Well, I'd love to have you join me for tea."

"I'll be right back with the tea . . . for two," Beatrice said curtly.

Sharlene shook her head. "And I thought it was cold outside. That woman is definitely not my biggest supporter," she observed ruefully.

Alice nodded. "I know, but don't take it personally. I don't think she's that crazy about me, either.

But she is Sally's grandmother, and I want them to be close."

"Can't she be close to Sally and still live somewhere else?" Sharlene commented in a wry tone as she took a seat on the flowered-chintz couch.

Alice lowered her voice. "Inviting her here might have been a mistake," she admitted. "Of course, she is a wonderful housekeeper . . ."

"But the living arrangements are becoming a little too strained?"

Alice shrugged and smiled. "There's not much I can do about that now, is there? And that's enough about my problems. How are you?" Alice studied Steven's sister, an attractive, dark-haired woman with a pixieish face. But despite Sharlene's ready smile, Alice nevertheless felt there was something very sad about her. Like Alice, she was a young widow, and losing her husband must have been devastating. But Alice sensed something else was bothering Sharlene. A part of her seemed closed off, as though it were protecting a deep and dark secret, but Alice didn't feel she could ask about it. The two women had grown close since Sharlene had moved in, but their relationship still did not include important confidences.

Sharlene kicked off her shoes. "I'm all right, I guess. A little tired."

"Are they working you too hard?" Alice asked with concern.

"No, actually I'm enjoying it. I get to do a little bit of everything, which I like."

"Steve would be so pleased that you and Willis

are working there. Sometimes it was hard for him to show how he felt about his family, but I know you were on his mind a lot."

"Growing up on that farm wasn't easy," Sharlene confessed. "Chadwell, Oklahoma, is no place to try to scratch out a living, and with all of us kids . . . it's a wonder we survived at all."

"Steve didn't have very fond memories of the place either," Alice agreed.

"His one goal in life was to get out of there." Sharlene paused, letting out a short laugh. "You know, he used to tell us stories about how he was going to be rich someday. Even as kids, we always believed him."

Just then, Beatrice bustled in with the tea service. "Don't you think I should call Sally inside?" she asked as she carefully placed the tray on the glass and wood coffee table.

Alice glanced at her watch. Only ten minutes had passed. "Why don't we give her a few more minutes."

"All right, if that's what you want," she said, shaking her head as she left the room.

As Alice poured tea for herself and Sharlene, she said, "What Beatrice doesn't realize is that it takes every bit of courage I can summon just to let Sally out of my sight. Ever since Steve died, I worry about everything."

"Really?" Sharlene asked, surprised. "You seem to be handling everything so well. When Joe was killed, I had nightmares for months. Sometimes, even during the day, it seemed like I couldn't catch my breath."

Alice looked at her sister-in-law with sympathy. "I know what you mean. The only thing that kept me going was that Sally needed me." She paused, then asked impulsively, "Sharlene, is it just Joe's death that's making you look so sad?"

Sharlene looked startled, then regained control. "Of course that's all. What else could it be? You of all people should know how I feel."

Alice immediately realized she'd overstepped her bounds and retreated. "You're right. Let's not even talk about it. Why don't you tell me what's happening at the office."

"What's happening?" Sharlene fiddled with a button on her sweater.

"You know, what's the gossip. I guess everyone is working hard on the shopping center project."

"Yes, they are."

"I think it's wonderful the way Willis has come in and carved out a niche for himself at the company."

Sharlene didn't know what to say. Before coming to Bay City, she hadn't seen Willis for years. Still, she remembered that even as a kid he had been very good at figuring out what he wanted and getting it . . . even if it belonged to someone else. Carving out a niche for himself was one way to put it, she supposed. She was tempted to tell Alice about her fears about Willis, but instead she just said, "Willis is spending a lot of time at the office. He works late almost every night."

Alice looked concerned. "I hope he isn't overdoing it. Do you think he needs more help down there?"

"No, that's not it. There are a couple of big projects on the boards, but I think we're handling it pretty well."

"You know, I've been feeling a little guilty about the business," Alice admitted. "When Steve left the company to me, I'm sure he didn't intend for me to be just a figurehead. I should really be thinking about taking a more active role at Frame Enterprises."

"But, Alice, you're a nurse."

"True, but I think I could learn the construction business. After all, look at you and Willis," she pointed out.

Before Sharlene could say any more, they were interrupted by squeals of laughter. They turned to see Sally being carried into the room on the shoulders of Russ.

"Look what I found outside," he called in a cheerful voice.

"Russ, what a nice surprise," Alice said, giving him a radiant smile. "To what do we owe the honor?"

He slid Sally off his shoulders and planted her on the floor. "Why shouldn't I come over and see my favorite girls?"

Alice noticed the smile that passed between Russ and Sharlene. "As much as you love me and your niece, I get the feeling you didn't come over to see us."

Russ turned his grin in Alice's direction. "Could be," he said mysteriously.

"Will you stay for dinner?"

"Sure. You don't have to go back to the office tonight, do you, Sharlene?"

"No," she replied. "Willis will be working late, but he said he didn't need any help."

"Good. Just because your brother's a workaholic doesn't mean you have to be."

Sharlene got up. "I think I'll go change my clothes," she said, anxious to get out of the room. The last thing she wanted to talk about was Willis's dedication to his job. She had her own ideas about why her brother was working so hard, and it wasn't for the good of the company. It was for the good of Willis Frame.

Mac loved to take walks in the evening. At dusk, when the busy pace of the day had slowed, he could stroll around the estate grounds mulling over the events of the day. Spring evenings were extra special because everything was just beginning to grow and blossom again. Before long, the flowers and bushes would be bursting into bloom.

As he walked across the lawn, Mac thought about how happy he was to be living in such a lovely house. He'd bought it for Rachel because when she was a girl it had been her fantasy house. She would stand out front, looking through the iron gates and dreaming about living there. Well, now she did, and Mac was delighted to have made one of her dreams come true.

He had known from the moment he met her that she was the woman he wanted by his side for the rest of his life.

Ironically, Iris had introduced them. Mac had sensed Rachel's spunk and spirit right away. Later he learned that she hadn't had an easy life.

Rachel was very honest with Mac about her past, but none of it mattered to him. He didn't see her scheming side; instead, he saw a strong yet frightened woman—someone whom love would temper and change. Whatever hurts Rachel had suffered in the past, Mac promised himself he would kiss or spend them away. He understood how important money and security were to Rachel, but that didn't bother him; he could offer her plenty of both. And that, he thought with satisfaction, was just what he had done.

Marriage to Mac had also given Rachel the added luxury of having time to work on developing her talents as a sculptor. In fact, he could hear the sound of her chisel as she chipped away at a block of marble in the makeshift studio he had had created for her in one of the mansion's back rooms.

That was the only tiny flaw in his happiness. When they were first married, they spent all their evenings together, cuddled up in front of the fire, or better yet, up in the bedroom. Now a good portion of Rachel's time was spent in her art room. Mac had to laugh. It would have been bad enough to have a young wife who wanted to go out dancing all the time. Instead, all his wife wanted to do was work.

He looked at his watch and noticed it was almost time for Robert to arrive. As much as Mac enjoyed Robert's company, he was pretty sure his visit had been suggested by Iris, and that concerned him. True to his word, he had not seen or spoken to Iris since their fight. He suspected Robert was coming over tonight to plead Iris's case.

The butler appeared at the French doors. "Mr. Cory, Mr. Delaney is here to see you."

"Thank you, Evans," Mac replied. As much as he wanted to put this visit off, he didn't think it was right to keep Robert waiting.

"Hello, Mac." Robert greeted his father-in-law as he appeared in the library.

"Hello, Robert. Can I offer you a drink?"

"Yes, please. A scotch and soda."

Mac went over to the portable bar and prepared drinks for each of them. "Cheers," he said after handing Robert his drink. "Well, let's sit down. I take it this isn't just a social call."

Robert looked uncomfortable as he settled himself into a red leather chair. "Frankly, Mac, I'm coming to you out of desperation. Iris has cried almost constantly since you went to see her, and I'm afraid she's going to make herself sick."

"And she told you she will never recover unless we reconcile."

"That's right." Robert nodded, a little surprised that Mac understood the situation so well. He had thought he was going to have to explain it all.

"Do you know what Iris did to cause me to become so angry with her?"

"Actually, I don't," Robert said with embarrassment. "Every time I tried to find out why she was so upset, she would just get hysterical. It seemed best if I talked to you." Robert leaned forward in his chair. "Maybe I can help work it out."

Mac sipped his drink. "I'm not surprised Iris hasn't told you the circumstances surrounding our estrangement, but frankly, I don't think it's my place to tell you."

"Why not?"

"It wouldn't change anything. I have no desire to make up with Iris, and consequently, there is no real reason for me to tell you what she's done."

"I'm sorry to hear that, Mac—" Before Robert could continue, the phone rang.

"Excuse me, please. I'm expecting a business call, so I have to get that. But please stay and finish your drink. We can talk some more when I'm finished."

Robert slumped into his chair. Alone in the wood-paneled library, he let his thoughts roam. He should have known better than to see Mac without first finding out the truth from Iris. The truth and Iris—those were two opposing concepts, he thought. The sweet, thoughtful Iris he had courted was a completely different person from the woman to whom he was now married. The longer he lived with her, the less he found he really knew her. Obviously, she had done something truly horrible if even Mac wanted nothing more to do with her. But what troubled Robert even more was that Iris had been playing games with him, using him as a pawn in her battle with her father. Well, not anymore. He was going to find out just what Iris had done to make Mac so mad at her. And she would have to be the one to tell him.

Chapter Three
Telling Truths

Marianne pulled into the parking lot of the dreary apartment building where her father was now living. With its crumbling paint and its litter-strewn lawn, the building hardly looked like a place where you'd find one of Bay City's most successful attorneys. She shut off the ignition, but didn't get out of the car. She needed a moment to collect herself, and plan what she was going to say to her father. In spite of her efforts to ignore them, Marianne knew her mother's words about sharing the blame for her parents' situation had been correct. Well, she reasoned, if she was responsible for her parents' breakup, it was up to her to see that they got back together. *I'll just have to persuade Daddy to go and talk to Mom,* she told herself. *I'm sure they can work it out.*

Knowing what she had to do, Marianne locked her car and made her way past the disinterested man at the desk and up to her father's apartment.

A disheveled John opened the door, and a look of surprise crossed his face. "Marianne, what are you doing here?"

"That's a nice way to greet your daughter," she answered lightly, giving him a little kiss on the cheek. "Aren't you going to ask me to come inside?"

"Of course," John said. "Uh, you'll have to forgive the way the place looks." He motioned her into the room.

Marianne looked around the messy apartment in shock. "Well, that's why I'm here," she said, taking off her raincoat and clearing some legal pads off a chair. "You know, there's no reason why you should be living here."

John's eyes swept over the dingy room. "I suppose you're right. I should probably start looking for another place, something more permanent."

"No you shouldn't," Marianne protested. "You should be at home, where you belong."

John ran a hand through his dark hair. "Now, honey, you know that's impossible."

"No, it's not. You and Mom belong together," she said firmly.

"I wish that could happen," he replied, sitting down across from her on an old wooden chair, "but too much has gone on between us."

"Dad," Marianne began, looking at her father earnestly, "I know I'm partly responsible for what's happened—"

"Don't say that—" John tried to interrupt.

"I have to," she insisted, "because it's true. I

know now that I shouldn't have made Mom promise not to tell you I was pregnant. It's just that I was so ashamed. You've always thought of me as your perfect little girl. . . ." Sobs made it impossible for her to say any more.

"Honey, please." Distressed, John took his daughter's hands in his. "It's all over now. I'm just sorry you had to go through such a terrible ordeal without me. I wish I could have been there for you."

"I know that now," Marianne sniffed. "Oh, Daddy, if you really want to put it all behind you, will you at least try to make up with Mom?"

He stood up and began pacing the floor, and she noticed he had the same distracted look on his face that her mother had had when she was discussing their estrangement.

"Sweetheart, there are some things you just don't understand about our separation."

"Like what?" she pressed.

John hesitated. He didn't want to tell her the whole truth, but there were some things he had to confess. "I said some terrible things to your mother."

Marianne waited silently for him to continue.

"I told her I wasn't surprised you had gotten pregnant considering her example. I said what else could we expect of our daughter when she had done the same thing at your age."

"Dad!" Marianne exclaimed, horrified.

"I know, I know. I realize now that it was an awful thing to say, but at the time I was hurt and angry. It just seemed to me like history was repeating itself, first with your pregnancy and then the abortion."

"No wonder Mom's been so upset," Marianne murmured. "What else did you say?"

It's not what I said, but what I did, John thought. Obviously, Pat had not given him away. If Marianne had known about his affair with Barbara, she never would have come to see him. Well, if Pat didn't think Marianne had to know, he certainly wasn't going to be the one to tell her. "Honey, a lot was said and done in the heat of anger. You know your mother and I have had problems on and off for years. I guess the stress of this incident was just the straw that broke the camel's back."

"See," she challenged, "it *was* my fault. And the only way I can ever live with myself is if you and Mom give it another chance."

John faced his daughter squarely. "I'm not sure that's possible."

"Well, it won't be if you don't try," she insisted stubbornly.

"What about Dave Gilchrist? He and your mother have grown quite close, haven't they?"

"Mom says they're just friends."

John looked at his daughter sitting across from him, so convinced and determined. He had to admit he was tired of living alone, away from his family, and his feelings for Pat were still very strong. In fact, thoughts of a reconciliation had been on his mind ever since Barbara left town. Perhaps Marianne was right; maybe there was hope after all. "All right, you win. I'll give it one more chance."

"You will?" she cried, throwing herself into his arms. "Thank you, Daddy."

"I'm not saying this will work," he said as he hugged her.

"I know, I know, but you'll never find out if you don't give it a shot."

He had to smile at his daughter's enthusiasm. "I'll give your mother a call."

"No way. You're going over there tonight."

"Tonight?" he repeated, "I don't think—"

"I know Mom's going to be home," Marianne urged. "I heard her say she was just going to curl up with a book."

"I suppose I could call and ask if she would see me."

"Don't call, Dad, just go over there."

John looked at his daughter with surprise. "You mean just barge in?"

"Mom might be surprised at first, but once she sees you there and realizes that you really want to make up with her, she'll be glad you came. Wait and see."

Two hours later, dressed in a suit and tie, with a bouquet of white roses on the seat beside him, John was driving toward the large, rambling house where he used to live.

He definitely had mixed feelings about what he was doing. His relationship with Pat was so complex and so tangled that John was no longer sure it could be sorted out. When things first started going sour, John had thought an affair with an attractive woman like Barbara was the way to forget about Pat. But now he could admit to himself that the whole time he was with Barbara, thoughts of Pat had always been in the back of his mind.

Yet there was no doubt that at some very basic level, he was angry with Pat, too. She should never have agreed to keep Marianne's pregnancy a secret from him. The major reason his affair with Barbara had happened was because John felt so estranged from his wife. The secrets between them had propelled him right into the arms of his associate.

John winced a little when he thought of Barbara. He hadn't really been very fair to her. At the very least, he should never have told her he'd asked Pat for a divorce when he hadn't. Still, he had loved her, John told himself. It was just that he had cared more for Pat.

He glanced at the roses, wrapped in green tissue paper, lying next to him. Pat had always loved white roses. John hoped she would see them as a symbol of their new relationship, one that would be based on honesty and trust. As Marianne had said, it was worth a shot.

Most of the lights were off at the house when John pulled up to the curb. Could Pat have gone out after all? he wondered. Or maybe she had decided to take her book upstairs to bed even though it was still quite early.

Grabbing the flowers, he hurried up the walk. He peered in through the picture window and although the living room was dark, he could see figures moving around the kitchen. It looked to be Pat and a man. John was about to ring the bell, but he thought better of it. The last thing he wanted to do was embarrass himself in front of a stranger.

John made his way to the back of the house, where he could see things more clearly through the windows. Sitting at the kitchen table, deep in conversation, were Pat and Dave. *Damn him,* John thought, tired of the good doctor always being in his way. Well, he certainly wasn't going to ring the bell now. He would just have to tell Marianne that he'd visit Pat some other night.

John was about to walk away when he noticed the kitchen door and window were slightly ajar. *You'll feel like a fool if you get caught,* he warned himself, but he couldn't resist the overpowering temptation to hear what Pat and Dave were talking about. After standing near the door for only a few seconds, he heard his name.

"I really appreciate your coming over here on such short notice," Pat was saying. "I just started thinking about this whole situation with Marianne and John, and I got so upset."

"Marianne's still hoping you and John will reconcile?" Dave asked softly.

She nodded. "Sometimes I wonder if he's putting her up to this. All she seems to talk about anymore is the two of us getting back together."

"I doubt if he's behind it. You have to remember that Marianne doesn't know about her father's affair. She thinks your estrangement from him is something that should be easily resolved."

Pat shook her head sadly. "If only she knew. First

that awful Bernice Kline, then Barbara. Some track record, huh?"

"I'm sorry you have to go through all of this," Dave said, putting his hand lightly over hers. "I wish I could do more to help."

"I was such a fool. I should have left him after I found out about Bernice." Pat let out a short, wry laugh. "Instead, I drank myself into a stupor. Well, that's all in the past. This time I'm not going to wallow in self-pity. I'm going to face up to the fact that my marriage is over and start making a new life for myself."

Dave studied Pat's face. "You and John have a long history together," he reminded her. "Do you really want to throw all that away?"

Pat looked out the kitchen window, at the very spot where John was standing, but she saw only shadows. "The truth is, I never should have married John. We were wrong for each other right from the start."

John couldn't bear to hear any more. He stuffed the roses into the garbage can, and left without a backward glance.

"You're kidding, right?" Michael looked at his twin sister in disbelief.

"No," Marianne assured him as she made herself at home in Michael's small apartment. "By tomorrow morning, Mom and Dad will have reconciled."

Michael took a seat on his secondhand sofa. "And then we'll all be one big, happy family again, I suppose," he said sourly.

"Well, you don't have to be so sarcastic about it. At least I'm trying to get them back together."

"So did I . . . once," he answered enigmatically.

"You did? When? While I was in Boston?"

"That's right. While you were having a grand old time, I was playing matchmaker."

"What happened?" she asked.

"Let's just say it didn't work out," Michael snapped.

Marianne could see it was a sore subject with her brother, but why? As much as she wanted to know the details, it was obvious that he didn't want to talk about it. "Don't feel bad," she said at last. "They probably just weren't ready for your help."

"And now I suppose they're ready for yours?" He let out a short, harsh laugh.

"Why are you acting like this," Marianne pressed. "You sound like you don't want them to get back together."

"They're adults. They can do whatever they want."

"Don't you think Mom and Dad would be happier if they made up?"

Michael got up and walked over to the desk. He flipped through some of the books that were on the desk, his face averted so Marianne couldn't read his expression. "No, I don't think Mom would be better off."

"But why not?" she asked, clearly puzzled.

Why, indeed? Michael knew that his mother didn't want her to be told about John's indiscretions, but he wondered if that was such a good idea. Sure, Marianne idolized their father, but that was part of the reason the trouble had started in the first place. Things would have been different if she had just leveled with him about her pregnancy. Still, Michael didn't especially want to be the one to tell his sister the truth.

"I'm waiting for an answer," she reminded him. "You can't just say you think Mom and Dad shouldn't be together and not give me a reason why."

"They're two separate people who have to live their own lives," he raged.

Marianne walked over to her brother. "But they shouldn't be. That's just it. They had a wonderful marriage."

"Will you stop being so naive! You know this isn't the first time they've lived apart."

"Well, I know Mom did some bad things in the past—"

"Mom?" he shouted. "Are you out of your mind? Everything that's happened has been Dad's fault," he cried, losing his temper completely.

"I don't think so," Marianne protested. "Dad's always been a perfect husband and father."

"Oh, right," Michael said bitterly.

"And frankly," Marianne continued, "I don't know how Mom can even look at Dr. Gilchrist. He doesn't even belong in the same room with Daddy."

"Maybe she thought it would be nice to have a man who was faithful to her for a change!" The words slipped out before Michael even knew he'd said them. As he looked into Marianne's shocked face, he knew he would have given anything to take them back.

"What do you mean by that?" she asked, looking a little pale.

"Nothing," Michael hedged as he backed into his bedroom. "Hey, I've got to go out tonight," he said, turning to take a clean shirt from his closet.

Marianne followed him and grabbed his arm. "Don't give me that garbage. What did you mean just then? Hasn't Dad been faithful to Mom?"

Michael searched his sister's eyes. "Do you really want to know the truth?"

"Yes, of course, I do."

"All right, then, I'll tell you. Why shouldn't you know? Sit down." He motioned to the bed. "You know, Marianne, you weren't the only one who wanted Mom and Dad to get back together. I did, too. I wanted it so much that I went over to Barbara's one night to see if I could get her to talk some sense into Dad. I got quite a surprise when I arrived," he said, his voice heavy with sarcasm.

"What?" Marianne asked, terrified to hear the answer.

"I saw our father there—in a compromising situation with Barbara."

Marianne clutched one of the throw pillows on Michael's bed. She felt as if she'd been punched in the stomach. "It can't be. You were mistaken. Not Barbara."

"I'm afraid so, sis," Michael said.

"Maybe they were . . ." Marianne floundered helplessly.

"Forget the excuses. It was just what it appeared to be. You know the ironic thing—I'd been hoping Barbara could help me convince Dad that he should go back home."

"Did you tell Mom?"

"She found out later," he said quietly. "Then she told me that this wasn't the first time Dad had had an affair. A while back, there was another woman, someone named Bernice Kline."

"No!" Marianne wanted to put her hands over her ears like a little child, but she knew it wouldn't help. "That's horrible!" she cried.

"I know."

Agitated, Marianne got up and began pacing the floor. "I can't believe this . . . my own father. I thought he was better than that."

"Well, he's not," Michael said flatly. "And I'm pretty angry at him, too, but I guess we just have to realize that these things happen."

Marianne stared at her brother, her eyes blazing. "What we have to realize is that we belong to a family of liars. Nobody tells anyone the truth anymore."

Michael stepped toward his sister and put his arm around her, but she backed away from him. "Leave me alone, Michael."

"Don't be that way," he said, holding on to her arm.

"Leave me alone." She wrestled out of his grasp. "I hate you, I hate you all." With that, she broke into sobs and ran out of the apartment.

Chapter Four
Disclosures

Carol sat hunched over her desk in the trailer at the shopping center site. When she was drawing up plans, she could sit happily at her desk all day. But going over columns of figures and price projections was an entirely different matter. As far as she was concerned, it was enough to drive anyone crazy.

Surely there was a mistake somewhere, Carol thought, rubbing her eyes. According to her calculations, the project was so far over budget that it was going to cost Frame Construction thousands and thousands of dollars in overruns. And if that was true, Willis was going to kill her.

Carol threw down her pencil and pulled off the jacket to her expensive linen suit. Then she walked over to the file cabinet and pulled out the blueprints for the project. Maybe there was some way she could still cut costs. She pored over the plans for a while, but then rolled them up and put them away. It was hopeless.

Walking over to the window of the trailer, she

observed the work that was going on outside. She knew that any day now Willis was going to ask her for the final cost estimate, and she had no idea what she was going to tell him. If she told him the truth, he was going to be furious. If there was one thing she couldn't stand, it was making Willis mad at her. Still, she didn't dare lie, either.

Oddly, when Carol had first started dating Willis, she'd done it to further her career. She could tell he was impressed by her cool, blond good looks and her wealthy, upper-class background. For her part, Carol figured a young architect who needed to talk her way into a job would find it easier to convince Willis of her talents if he had a personal interest in her success. She made sure that interest developed quickly.

But a strange thing happened to Carol once she was employed at Frame Enterprises: she found her situation with Willis was slowly turning around. The affection she had faked became very real. She couldn't wait each morning until Willis arrived at the office. If he stayed late, so did she. He was a magnetic, ambitious man, and Carol had fallen totally under his spell. She knew that someday he would take over the whole company, and she was ready to help him in any way that she could.

"Hey, sunshine," a voice suddenly called. "How come you're standing there looking out the window?"

Carol turned around to see Willis standing in the doorway of the trailer. His tight, muscular body was well outlined under his flannel shirt. With deep-set eyes and a thin, almost cruel mouth, Willis could not be called conventionally good-looking. There was, however, an element of danger in him—like a wild animal ready to spring—that Carol found surprisingly appealing. He was different from the coddled rich boys she'd known before.

"Oh, hello, Willis."

He walked over to her and gave her a hard, fast kiss. Then he drew back and looked at her with concern. "You look upset. Is there some problem?"

"No, uh, not really. Just a few things I want to check out." Carol knew that the time had come to mention the overrun problem to Willis, but she had to do it with the utmost care. She hoped that if she gave him the bad news outside, with so many people milling around, he would have to keep his furious temper in check. "Let's go for a walk."

"Sure. I wanted to check the beams over in the northeast corner anyway."

They left the trailer and went out onto the construction site, which was a storm of activity. Men carried pipe fittings, carpenters hammered away, heavy machinery hummed in the background: all this greeted them as they made their way around the site. It was a big, dirty, noisy place and both Carol and Willis loved it.

"Look at that." Willis pointed with pride to the frame of the parking garage. "There'll be space for a thousand cars there," he said happily. He looked as proud as a father watching a baby take its first steps.

"It's wonderful. This is going to be the most exciting shopping complex Bay City has ever seen." Carol hoped that if she could keep his enthusiasm up, he'd take the bad news in his stride.

"It should be. A great architect designed it," he said, stepping over some wires.

"The design is great," she agreed, spotting an opportunity to tell him the bad news, "but it's going to cost a little more than we thought." The last words came out in a rush.

He stopped and looked at her with narrowed eyes. "Exactly what does that mean?"

Carol took a deep breath. "I've been going over the figures all morning. I can't give you the exact numbers, but it looks as though the overruns are going to be bad."

"How bad?"

She just shook her head, but the defeated expression on her face was enough to tell him that the problem was serious.

"How could you let this happen?" he demanded, his voice shaking with anger.

Carol was frightened, but she tried to stand her ground. "This isn't all my fault. You knew I didn't know much about budgeting, and as project manager you have a certain responsibility—"

"Forget it," he cut in forcefully. "The budget was your job and apparently you've messed it up." A few workers turned in his direction and looked at him curiously. He lowered his voice a little. "Now, what are you going to do about it?"

When she didn't reply, he stood stock-still and said angrily, "How are you going to correct this problem?"

She gave a helpless little shrug. "What can I do?"

He thought for a minute. "I have an idea."

"What is it?" she asked anxiously.

"You can cover the cost of the overruns yourself."

Carol couldn't believe she'd heard him correctly. "Cover them myself? You've got to be kidding."

"I'm not," he assured her. "You've made a mistake, now you've got to pay for it."

"But, Willis," she protested, bewildered, "that's not the way it works. The company has to absorb the loss, not the architect."

He looked as though he might slap her. "This one does. I am not going to have Vic Hastings find out that this project is over budget. How do you think that will look?" he asked, raising his voice once more. "How will *we* look?"

They were starting to draw some attention, so Carol pulled Willis off to the side of a tool shed where they could have some privacy. "I know it won't look very good, but Vic would understand. He's a very nice person."

"He's a nice person," he mimicked her. "Vic is running a company that by rights belongs to me, and if he can get rid of me, he will."

"I don't believe that."

"I don't care what you believe," he barked. "I've come up with a solution, and we're lucky I did."

"But . . . we're talking about a lot of money here."

"Then it's a good thing that you have a lot of money, isn't it?" He began walking again and propelled her along with him. "I want you to get to

57

the bank this afternoon. The sooner the better, in fact. I want you to deposit the amount you think the overrun will be, plus a little bit more to cover any other mistakes. You'll do that for me, won't you?" His voice was more pleasant now.

Carol knew there was no point in arguing. Making Willis happy was all that really mattered to her. "Yes," she finally sighed. "I'll do it."

"That's my girl." He gave her a confident smile. "Soon this will all be settled and no one will be the wiser."

Jim Matthews looked over the figures one more time. He had been an accountant for more years than he cared to remember, but he always gave everything a second look. This held doubly true when it was his daughter's business he was auditing.

John sat across the desk from Jim and looked at him with affection. When this current trouble had first started between him and Pat, he wondered if he and his father-in-law would be able to continue working together for Frame Enterprises. But it had been surprisingly easy, and John attributed that to the fact that Jim was a gentleman. He loved his family but didn't judge or condemn other people. So John had continued handling Frame's legal affairs, and Jim kept doing the books.

Jim took off his glasses and tapped them against the desk for a moment, then spoke. "I've looked at these numbers again and again, and as far as I can see, there's a big problem with the shopping center project."

"What do you mean?" John questioned.

"Well, this set of books hasn't been kept very well. I may not have all the figures here."

"But you think the overruns are large?"

"I'm fairly sure. I don't see how they can make up that much money this late into the construction, either."

John glanced at the papers the older man handed him. "Then Vic was right."

Jim nodded. "Vic didn't know exactly what was wrong with the project when he called me because Willis and Carol have been playing it pretty close to the vest. But from the little information he had, Vic did pick up on the fact that something was amiss."

"Now what? Do you want to tell Alice?" John asked.

He shook his head. "I hate to bother her," he said slowly. "She's just getting her life back together. Besides, she's such a big fan of Willis's. I don't want to disillusion her unless it's necessary."

"She was so pleased when he came into the company," John agreed. "I guess she sees his presence as a way to carry on Steve's legacy in the construction business. Too bad it's not turning out that way."

"Well, the boy wasn't all that experienced. And just because he and Carol have gotten into a bit of hot water with this project doesn't mean they should be fired for it," Jim protested, trying to be fair.

"No, no, I didn't mean anything like that. We

could let Vic handle it, I suppose, but I do think Alice should be told. She did ask us to let her know if we found anything."

He thought for a moment. "You're right. Do you want to go over there tonight and talk to her about it?"

"I don't think so," John said, glancing at his watch. "Not tonight, anyway. Marianne is coming over."

"That's nice," Jim replied with a kind smile.

An uncomfortable look passed over John's face. "This is the second time in two days that she's asked to come over."

"Don't you want to see her?" Jim asked, his smile turning to a frown.

"Of course I do. It's just that she sounded so strange when she called earlier today. You know, she really wants Pat and me to get back together."

"Is there any chance of that?" the older man asked bluntly.

John looked at his father-in-law and shook his head slowly. "I don't think so. I'm sorry."

"Well, a divorce isn't what I would have wanted for you two, but I know you'll do what you think is right."

"It'll be hard on Marianne," John added, remembering his daughter's recent visit. She was probably wondering why he hadn't shown up at the house the previous night, and he didn't know what he was going to tell her.

"Yes, you're going to have to be very gentle with her," Jim agreed. "She loves you so much."

"I know."

"Well," he said, rising, "since you're tied up tonight, I'll just have to go see Alice myself. I think I'll give her a call right now; the sooner she finds out about this, the better, I guess."

Beatrice carefully wrote down the message as she hung up the phone. If there was one thing she was precise about, it was making sure people got their messages. She was putting the note on Alice's desk when Sally came bounding in to the study.

"Hi, Grandma. Who called?"

"Alice's father, dear. He's going to stop by tonight."

"Grandpa's coming!" Sally cried joyfully. Jim was one of her favorite people.

Beatrice gritted her teeth. If anything irked her more than hearing Alice addressed as Mommy, it was Jim getting the title "Grandpa."

"Yes, he'll be here after supper," she said, trying to hide her irritation from the child.

Sally cocked her head. Despite Beatrice's best efforts, the perceptive child had picked up the annoyance in her grandmother's voice. "Don't you like Grandpa?"

"Certainly, I do," Beatrice replied quickly. This was no lie. She did like Jim, she even found him attractive in a way. That still didn't make him Sally's grandfather as far as she was concerned. "I think I'll bake some cookies for his visit," she said briskly, changing the subject. "Would you like to help me?"

61

"No, I'm going to go out and feed the ducks down by the pond," she said, grabbing her jacket from the desk chair where she'd left it.

Beatrice was horrified. "By the pond? Alone? I won't hear of it."

"Mom says I can as long as I'm careful."

"You must have misunderstood her," Beatrice countered. "She wouldn't let you go near the pond by yourself."

"I'm not going to fall in," Sally said scornfully.

"No, you're not, because I'm certainly not letting you out until I get this straightened out with Alice. And no pouting, young lady. We'll have just as much fun making cookies. Now, into the kitchen."

What could Alice be thinking of, Beatrice wondered for the hundredth time. *Doesn't that woman have any sense at all?*

The shrill sound of the phone interrupted her thoughts. "If that's Alice calling from the car repair shop, I'm going to give her a piece of my mind," she muttered, answering sharply, "Hello?"

"Mom?" The voice on the other end of the phone sounded very far away.

"Raymond, is that you?"

"Yes, Mom."

"Where are you calling from?" she asked, sitting down.

"I'm still in California, but I won't be here for long," he replied mysteriously.

"Are you leaving on a trip?"

"Not exactly . . ." Ray said, the noise of a passing car drowning out the rest of his words.

Beatrice pressed the phone more closely to her ear. "What?"

"I'm not going on vacation; I'm coming to Bay City."

"But, Ray, you were just here for a visit a little while ago," she pointed out, suddenly fearful. "Is something wrong?"

"I'm afraid so. Olive and I are splitting up. It's been a possibility for a long time, but we both decided that now's the time to make the break."

"And the boys?" Beatrice asked with a catch in her throat.

"Olive and the boys are going to stay here in California. I, however, need a change of scene, and I thought it would be nice to be near you and Sally."

Beatrice's thoughts were whirling. "That sounds nice, Ray, but—"

"Will you make a reservation for me at the Beverly Hotel? I'll probably be there on the twelfth."

"Certainly, son. How long do you think you'll be staying? I'll need to let the hotel know."

Ray paused. "Leave it open-ended, Mom. I may be staying permanently." She didn't say anything. "Well, this is costing me a bundle, so I'd better hang up. Thanks for taking care of the hotel."

"You're welcome. I'll see you soon." Slowly, Beatrice hung up the phone. She sat quietly for a moment as she absorbed her son's news. She wasn't terribly upset about the divorce since she'd never much cared for Olive. As for the boys, well, that was too bad. Still, maybe Ray would get custody.

She'd make sure he fought for it, anyway. But what really puzzled Beatrice was why Ray was coming to Bay City of all places. She could understand his coming for a visit, maybe, but for good? Ray was always crowing about that California sunshine; why would he suddenly want to come back to the Midwest?

"Hi, Beatrice, I'm home," a cheerful voice called.

Beatrice turned and saw Alice in the doorway, a bright smile on her face. Suddenly, everything clicked. There was a reason why Ray was coming back to Bay City, and her name was Alice Frame.

Taking his keys out of his pocket, Robert opened the door to his home. Even though he was an architect, he thought as he stepped into the elegant room, there was no doubt about who was responsible for the decor. As beautifully appointed as the living quarters were, they were all Iris. Robert had never felt comfortable there. If the truth were told, he was equally uncomfortable in his marriage. He walked to the marble fireplace, over which hung a beautiful portrait of Iris. He stared at it, as he often did when he was alone, thinking again that the artist had captured his wife at her loveliest and most inviting. That was one side of the woman he had married, but there was a darker, more disturbing side as well. Unfortunately, he never knew which side he was going to have to deal with. It made life very difficult.

He walked over to the bar and fixed himself a drink. Iris had been out of town for a few days, still trying to recover from her fight with her father. She had been horribly disappointed to hear from Robert that Mac was sticking to his decision not to see her again. Robert had tried to get the truth about their fight out of her right then, but she had pleaded a headache and gone to bed. By the time he returned from work the next day, she was gone, leaving only a scribbled note that said she just had to get out of Bay City for a while. He hadn't heard a word from her since.

Sitting down, Robert sipped his drink and tried to decide what he would do about dinner. He just couldn't face another meal alone. As he was calling John to see if he wanted to eat at Tall Boys, however, he heard the sound of a key in the door.

"Hello, Robert," Iris said. She barely looked at him as she made her way toward the bedroom, her garment bag over her arm and her night case in hand.

He followed her up the stairs and through the gold-trimmed double doors. "That's not much of a greeting after being gone for so long, is it?"

She gave him a hurried peck on the cheek but still would not look him in the eye. "Sorry, dear, I'm just very tired." Slowly, she began to unpack, hanging up several dresses.

"Iris, how unlike you," Robert said, taking a long sip of his drink. "Isn't unpacking something your maid usually does?"

Iris sat down at the edge of her bed and sighed. "Please, don't be sarcastic. I'm simply not up to it."

"Aren't you even going to tell me where you went?" he asked, his voice soft.

"New York," she said briefly. "I thought it would make me feel better."

"And did it?"

"Not especially," she admitted.

"So what's next?" he said, looking down at her. She was such a pitiful sight that he was starting to feel sorry for her.

Finally, she raised her eyes to look at him. "I don't know. I've got to get Daddy's love back somehow. I just have to."

"What happened between you and Mac? You never really told me anything."

Robert's probing question was enough to get Iris moving. Quickly, she hopped up and continued her unpacking. In an agitated voice, she said, "What difference does it make? It's all water under the bridge anyway."

"Apparently not. Not if Mac still refuses to speak to you," he said gently.

"That will change. It has to. My father and I are very close, and nothing could come between us. You know that."

Robert put his arm around her shoulder and led her across the bedroom to the little sitting area. "I know that you've always wanted your father's love, and sometimes it was difficult for you to get it. But I don't understand—"

Iris rubbed her temples distractedly. "I just don't understand why Daddy is choosing Rachel over me," she interrupted.

"Is that how you see it?" He was shocked.

"How else can I see it?" she snapped. "She

makes some silly accusations against me and suddenly my father isn't speaking to me anymore."

Robert thought he was finally getting somewhere. "What accusations?"

Getting up from the love seat, Iris nervously picked up her hairbrush and started brushing her hair. "I don't remember."

He followed her to her dressing table and looked at her in the mirror. "I don't believe that. You must remember."

"No . . . no, I don't," she denied.

After turning her around until she was facing him, he said, "You've made up lies about Rachel and she's caught you, is that it?"

"Robert, I tell you it's all nonsense. She thinks I had something to do with her miscarriage, or something equally ridiculous."

"But, how could you have had anything to do with her miscarriage."

"I couldn't, of course, but Rachel blames me anyway. She says that she called here the night she miscarried, trying to reach Mac."

"And did she?" Robert pressed.

Once more, Iris could not meet her husband's gaze. "I don't remember."

Oh, God, he thought. This was worse than he'd ever dreamed. He searched his brain trying to remember if Rachel had called her that evening, but it was all a blur. "Iris, that was a horrible thing to do," he finally said in a hushed voice.

"Are you taking Rachel's part, too?" She began crying.

"I don't want to."

"Then don't," she said, sobbing harder. "Is it my fault if Rachel thinks she called here? The woman was delirious for days after the miscarriage. How could she possibly remember something like a little telephone call?"

Robert was at a loss. Obviously, there was more to this story than she was telling him, but she was so distraught that he could hardly keep questioning her. "Iris, you're tired and upset. Why don't you lie down and take a nap for a while. If you want, we can go out for some dinner later."

She slowly nodded her head in agreement. Like a little child she stretched out on her bed, pulling a comforter over her slight body, and closed her eyes.

Deep in thought, Robert looked at her for a moment, then shut off the light and left the room.

Chapter Five
Marianne's Rage

Marianne knew that she shouldn't be going over the same things again and again, but she just couldn't help herself. She sat in her room with the curtains drawn, and she rocked back and forth in her Grandma Mary's wooden rocker.

Staring into space, she replayed the events of the previous night in her mind. Her father had obviously been expecting a cheerful visit from his little girl, but Marianne's fury was fighting with her indignation when she'd stormed through his door. Once more, she remembered the awful scene. . . .

"Hello, darling," he had greeted her. He even gave her a small kiss, but all he received in answer was a dirty look and stony silence.

Following Marianne into his small living room, her father waited to see what was on her mind. Finally, she turned to him, her eyes blazing. "I asked you last night if you wanted to get back together with Mom, and you said there were things about the situation I didn't understand."

"That's right," he answered, feeling more and more uncomfortable.

"I want you to explain those things to me."

He busied himself with picking up his shirts and straightening up his papers. "Marianne, that's really between your mother and me."

"Michael knows," she said flatly.

He shuddered. "Knows what?"

Marianne stared at her father coldly. "He knows why Mom is so angry with you."

John looked up from his nervous tidying, a shocked look on his face.

"Don't look so surprised. Surely you remember Michael coming to visit Barbara and finding you in her arms. It doesn't seem like the kind of meeting you could forget easily."

"Sarcasm doesn't become you, Marianne."

"Oh, and I suppose infidelity becomes you," she countered bitterly.

"I'm not making excuses for myself, but I do have an explanation."

"Which is?" she prompted.

"I felt your mother had betrayed me by not confiding in me," he began. "The more distance there was between your mother and me, the closer I became to Barbara."

"And then you went to bed with her."

"Yes," he admitted, "I . . . thought I loved her."

"And did you?"

"In a way, I suppose. Not like I loved your mother."

Marianne tried to contain her fury. "Now, let

me see if I've got this straight: you loved Barbara —or maybe you didn't—but you had an affair with her anyway. And you betrayed my mother in the process. I think this is all pretty pathetic, don't you?"

John had never felt so helpless in his life. He loved his little girl so much, and this was just the sort of ugliness he had wanted to spare her. "Who told you all this? Your mother?"

She looked at him with disbelief. "Mom? You've got to be kidding. In spite of all you've done to her, Mom is still as loyal as ever. She hasn't said a single word against you."

"That's good of her," John said with feeling.

"What's the difference? It's all coming out now," she snapped.

John sat down heavily on the tattered sofa that had come with the apartment. "Yes, I suppose it is." He paused. "Michael told you all of this, didn't he?"

Marianne didn't want to get her brother into trouble, but she didn't deny her father's accusation. "He didn't want to."

"Why would he tell you such a thing?" John exploded.

"Because it's the truth," she shouted back. "Although I'm not sure you would understand that concept."

"Sweetheart, try to understand," John pleaded. He was desperately upset at the transformation he was seeing before him. The hardened, embittered young woman confronting him was nothing like his Marianne, and it was all his fault.

Ignoring his distress, his daughter relentlessly pursued her questioning. "If you *can* be honest, tell me this: was Barbara the first woman you ever had an affair with?"

John didn't know where to look; he couldn't look at Marianne. Pictures of Bernice Kline flashed through his mind.

"Don't bother answering," she said in an icy tone. "The answer is written all over your face." She grabbed her purse and started to run out of the apartment, but John leaped up and grabbed her arm.

"Please, if we could just talk about this . . ."

"Talk about this?" she asked incredulously. "I don't want to talk about anything with you anymore." Marianne pulled herself away. "I don't know how I could have been so blind. I thought you were the most wonderful father in the world, but now I find out you're nothing but a liar and a cheater. Leave me alone from now on, okay? Just leave me alone."

Before her father could say anything else, Marianne had raced out the door. . . .

Now, as she continued rocking in her chair, she unsuccessfully tried to push the awful pictures out of her mind. They were firmly etched there, and she supposed they always would be. More than most girls, Marianne had thought her father was infallible. She even used to wonder if she would ever find a man as fine as he was. *What a joke*, she thought now. *What a stupid, cruel joke.*

A knock at the bedroom door interrupted her thoughts. She tried to ignore it, but the noise continued. "Go away, Mom," she called sharply. Her mother had been up to see her several times since the previous night. Obviously, her father had called and told her the whole story. Well, Marianne didn't want to see either one of them. She wished they'd just leave her alone.

"Marianne, open up. It's me, Michael."

"Go away."

"I'm not going anywhere." He rapped heavily on the door. "Come on, open this door or I swear I'll kick it down."

Marianne closed her eyes and sighed. He'd probably do it. She rose from her chair and opened the door. The bright hallway light hurt her eyes and she used one hand to shade them. "Michael, I really don't feel like seeing anyone right now."

He brushed past her and into the room. A disturbing scene met his eyes: Marianne in an old flannel robe, the curtains drawn, her clothes scattered on the floor where she had left them. "So, what are you going to do?" he asked. "Stay locked in this room for the rest of your life?"

Marianne sat down on her bed and refused to look at her brother. "Maybe."

"That's terrific," he said sarcastically. "If you want my opinion, I think it's time you came back to the land of the living."

"Oh, you do, do you?" she challenged, turning her head in his direction. "Well, maybe I don't want to. Maybe I'm not too interested in what goes on there. As far as I can see, it's just lots of dirty little lies and illicit affairs."

"Come on, sis," Michael said gently, stepping in front of her so she couldn't ignore him. "I know finding out about Dad was hard on you, but you've got to get past it."

"Sorry, Michael, I guess I'm not like you. I can't just ignore the things that are going on around me," she said bitterly.

"It wasn't all that easy for me," he pointed out. "How do you think I felt, finding Dad with Barbara?"

For the first time since her confrontation with her father, Marianne considered someone else's feelings. "It couldn't have been too easy," she said slowly.

Michael sat down on the bed next to his sister. "It was awful. You were away and I was here all alone to decide what to do."

"What did you do?" she asked seriously.

"At first, I went a little crazy," he admitted. "After I left Barbara's, I wandered around for a few hours. I can't even remember where I went." He proceeded to tell her about the rest of the night and the next few days of torment. "Anyway, I guess Mom walked in on the same scene I did a few days later."

Marianne was horrified. "She saw Dad and Barbara together?"

Michael nodded. "I found her locked in her room, just like you are now. She didn't want to see anyone either, so I called Dr. Gilchrist, and eventually he made her see reason."

It took Marianne a moment to digest all this information. Then she said, "Didn't anyone think that I should be told about this little news bulletin?"

Her brother shrugged helplessly. "You were away. When you got back . . . well, Mom and I know how you feel about Dad."

"Felt," she stated flatly.

"We just didn't want to hurt you if we didn't have to."

She looked into her brother's eyes sharply. "Nice sentiment, but that's not how I see it."

"How do you see it?" Michael asked, taken aback by the anger in his twin's voice.

"You betrayed me. Just like everyone else I've ever loved."

"Come on, Marianne, cut the dramatics."

"Dramatics?" she cried, her voice trembling dangerously. "Is that what you think this is? I find it hard to just ignore the fact that my father, who I always looked up to and admired, has been having an affair with his law partner, and you think I'm being dramatic? What should I do, throw a party?"

"Of course not," Michael said, equally upset now, "but do we have to——"

"Yes, we do," she broke in. "Let's see, who else has betrayed me? Well, there was Barbara. When I needed someone to talk to about wanting an abortion, who did I confide in? None other than dear old Barbara Weaver, that's who. I told her a lot, and she repaid my trust by ruining my parents' marriage." She shook her head sadly. "And the worst of all was Chris. He was going to marry me. We were going to be a family: me, Chris and the baby. . . ."

Michael wanted desperately to stop his sister, but he didn't know how. Maybe it was better if she just got everything out.

"Now I find out that even you and Mom were locked in a little conspiracy against me, a plot to keep me from finding out what kind of a man my dad really is."

"It wasn't like that, Marianne," her brother tried to explain.

She stood up and walked nervously around the room, ignoring her brother.

"Come on, sis, let's go downstairs. I'll fix you something to drink, something warm . . ."

"I don't want anything to drink. I want to be left alone."

He got up and put his hands on his sister's shoulders. "I can't stand seeing you like this."

She wearily rubbed her eyes. "Please, just go away."

"All right," he said, realizing he was losing the battle, at least for now. "But I'll be back. You can't stay here forever."

Dejected, he made his way downstairs. His sister was so sensitive. She always had been, even as a child. He had always been there to help her, to wipe away her tears, but this time he felt helpless.

"How is she?" his mother asked the moment Michael walked into the living room.

He shook his head. "Not too good."

"She's still upset with your father?"

"With all of us," he sighed. "She thinks we all lied to her, everyone from Chris to you, me and Dad. Even Barbara."

"Oh, dear." Pat stood up and walked over to the stairs. "Maybe I should try to talk to her again."

"I don't think so, Mom. Marianne is going to have to come to terms with her feelings by herself."

Pat turned and looked at her son with disbelief. "You don't mean that we should just let her stay up there?"

He went over to his mother and led her away from the staircase. "I don't know what else we can do. She won't listen to me, and I don't think she's going to listen to you, at least not now."

"You're right. Pretending that Marianne will talk to me is wishful thinking." Pat sat down heavily on the couch. "You know, when you told me you'd let it slip about John and Barbara, I was almost glad. It doesn't make me very proud to say this, but I thought that if she knew the truth, Marianne might not see me as the villain anymore. Maybe she would understand why I was so cold to your father."

"But you don't think she's going to feel that way?" Michael asked sympathetically, as he took a chair across from his mother.

"No, she's just as hostile to me as she was before. When she came home last night, before she rushed to her room, she told me how angry she was at both your father and me. She claims that we blamed her pregnancy and abortion for the problems we were already having in our marriage." Pat looked at her son with troubled eyes. "Do you think that's true? Were Marianne's troubles just an excuse for your father and me to move further apart?"

Michael didn't know what to say. Finally, he

answered, "I don't know, Mom. Does a child really ever know what's happening in his parents' relationship?"

"I shouldn't have put you on the spot like that," Pat quickly apologized. "I'm sorry, honey."

"Please, Mom, don't worry about me."

"I won't," she said with a grateful smile. "All I know is, Marianne's feelings haven't softened much towards me. I wonder if they ever will," she added quietly, more to herself than to her son.

At her words, Michael began feeling as though he were suffocating. He knew he should stay and comfort his mother, but he just had to get out of the house. "I'm going out for a while, Mom," he said, rising. "I'll stop in on my way home if the lights are still on."

Pat glanced at her watch. "I thought you could stay a little longer."

"I've just got to get out. I can't stand being here, knowing that Marianne is miserable and I can't do anything about it."

Pat sighed. "I know what you mean."

"Maybe I'll see you later." He kissed her cheek.

"Yes, come back if you're not too tired. In the meantime, I guess I'll just leave Marianne alone. Obviously, I'm the last person she wants to talk to."

Michael left and, after getting into his car, started driving aimlessly around town. It was almost nine-thirty, a little late for anything to be open in town except for the fanciest restaurants. Then he remembered that the student union at the university was open until eleven. It had just the kind of atmosphere he was looking for: noisy, crowded, a place where he wouldn't have to think for a while.

As he suspected, the union was jumping. It was so crowded that after he bought some fries and a milkshake, he couldn't find a place to sit down.

Just as he was getting ready to take his food outside and eat it on one of the stone benches that surrounded the union, he noticed Darrell Stevens sitting at a back booth, his head buried in a book. They had been in a number of classes together in the past, and Michael had always liked Darrell. He made his way over to his friend, who looked up.

"Hey, Mike, how's it going?" Darrell asked, his friendly eyes looking out through horn-rimmed glasses. "Have a seat."

Mike slid into the scarred wooden booth, which had been carved with the initials of long-ago sweethearts. "Reading something good?" he asked, gesturing toward Darrell's book. "You sure looked involved."

Darrell held up the heavy volume. "Yeah, it's great. Introduction to Chemistry. It's all about these elements who meet, fall in love, and form a compound."

Michael laughed at the corny joke. "Gee, I hope it has a happy ending."

"Getting a C in this class would be a very happy ending, but I doubt it's going to happen," he sighed.

"Having trouble with it?"

"I'm in Dalton's class," Darrell explained.

"Enough said." Hard-nosed Mr. Dalton had a

reputation for being especially hard on his first-year students.

"I wish I could help you, but I got through chem by the skin of my teeth myself."

Darrell took a sip of his Coke. "So what's happening with you, Mike. I haven't seen you around in a while."

Michael turned somber. "I've been busy with family problems, I'm afraid."

"Nothing serious, I hope," Darrell asked, the concern obvious in his voice.

"It is kind of serious, but I just don't feel like getting into it right now."

"Sure, I understand." He hesitated before adding, "Just tell me one thing—is Marianne okay?"

Michael remembered how interested Darrell had been in Marianne a while back. At the time, however, she had been completely caught up in her relationship with Chris. His sister certainly would have been much better off if she had paid some attention to Darrell, he thought.

Suddenly, he did feel like confiding in Darrell. He wasn't going to give away any of Marianne's secrets, but he could talk about the family's troubles in a general way. Darrell was a great guy, someone who obviously still cared about Marianne, and maybe that's what she needed right now.

Michael played with the straw in his milkshake, twirling it around. Finally, he decided just to plunge in. "Actually, Darrell, Marianne is going through a pretty rough time right now. And no, she's not okay."

Chapter Six
In Willis's Way

"Vic, you don't really think I'm going over your head, do you?" Alice asked with concern. "That's the last thing I'd do."

Vic's large, capable hands touched the top of his desk as he leaned forward. "This is your company. You can do whatever you feel is appropriate."

She gave him a probing look. "That's not an answer to my question."

Vic took a few seconds to decide what to say. "Frankly, I'm just as happy to have you deal with Willis directly. You gave him the shopping center project and Willis made it very clear that he didn't want my interference, so I think any discussion of problems should be between you and him. I'd just as soon stay out of it."

"But . . ." Alice said, looking troubled. "Are you angry with me, Vic?" She was very fond of the lanky, dark-haired man who had been running Frame Construction since Steven's death. It hadn't been easy coming to see him today, but after her father told her about the overruns, she knew it was time to check things out for herself. Still, since Vic was in charge of the company, Alice felt it was appropriate to talk with him before she spoke to Willis. He was also the one who told her there might be a problem, which was why she'd called her father in to look at the books in the first place.

Vic had refused to join Alice and Willis at lunch, where she planned to discuss the issue. It was apparent from his words and manner that Willis wasn't one of Vic's favorite people, and Alice was at a loss as to how to deal with the difference in their feelings about Willis. It would hurt her deeply if a rift were developing between them because she wanted Willis to have a role in his brother's company.

Vic pulled out his pipe, lit it and took a thoughtful puff. "No, I'm not angry. You know I think Willis is a very capable young man. But he seems a little . . . overeager to me."

"Steve would be pleased that Willis is working so hard," Alice maintained.

"I'm sure he would. But if Steve were here, Willis would also understand that his brother was the boss."

"Willis knows you're in charge," she scoffed.

"I'm not quite sure that he sees it that way," Vic said, puffing on his pipe.

She looked surprised. "Why do you say that?"

"It's hard to explain," he replied slowly. "I just feel that Willis thinks that because his last name is

Frame, he should be in charge. He sees me as some sort of usurper."

"Then this is another thing I'll have to bring up with him at lunch."

Thinking that would be a mistake, Vic said, "Please don't. I wouldn't want Willis to think I'm telling tales out of school, so to speak. As long as he runs his projects and I run mine, we should be able to make this association work."

"So, what you're saying is that although you're technically in charge, Willis's special relationship to the company has been causing problems."

"That about sums it up, yes," he replied.

"Then let me tell you about an idea I've been toying with," she began. "I haven't made any final decisions yet, but what would you think if I came to work here at the office?"

"You're considering doing that?" Vic blurted out, surprised.

"Yes, I think so. I feel as if it would be the right thing for me and for Frame."

He gave her a pleased smile. "Why, I think that's terrific. It could work out very well for all of us."

"I agree. After all, I am president of the company. I think it's high time I did more than just put my signature on pieces of paper."

"And I think Steven would have wanted you to take an active role in company affairs, too," Vic put in with a smile.

"I don't know how useful I'd be at first," Alice warned, "but I'm sure I could learn. And if I were here every day, the company would at least have a visible president."

"It all sounds good to me. When do you want to start?"

"Whoa," she cried, putting up her hands. "A lot of things have to be settled before I make my final decision. I just wanted to test the waters," she explained.

"Please consider it seriously," Vic told her. "I think it's an excellent idea, and if you decide to do it, you'll have my complete support."

Willis groaned inwardly. All he needed was Alice messing around the office all day. *Keep smiling,* he told himself. *You can't let Alice find out you think her plan stinks.* Willis flashed her his most disarming grin. "What an interesting idea," he finally said, his voice dripping with sincerity. "I hardly know what to say." In an effort to avoid saying anything right away, he flagged down a passing waiter and asked for the dessert menu.

While Willis gave his instructions to the waiter, Alice took a sip of water, and tried to gauge what he'd meant by "interesting." She had hoped that taking him out to lunch would make it easier to talk about the overruns. So far, however, she had not found the courage to bring it up. Instead, she began chattering nervously about her plan for spending more time at the office and taking a more active role at Frame. Willis hadn't seemed too enthusiastic, so the ever-insecure Alice covered by saying, "Of course, I haven't really decided yet."

"It's a big decision," he agreed. "Not something you ought to rush into."

"No, but I want to decide soon. If I do go ahead with my plans, there are arrangements that need to be made."

"I thought all of your work experience was in nursing," he remarked, looking at her with feigned interest. "Have you been involved in corporate work, too?"

"Not really," Alice admitted. "But I was a nurse supervisor and I think that kind of experience transfers over," she added, a trifle defensively.

There was a long silence. "I guess so," he finally said.

"I gather you don't much care for my plan," Alice observed, starting to feel hurt at his lack of confidence in her abilities.

Willis gave his sister-in-law a small smile. "I don't really care one way or the other. It's up to you to decide what you want to do about work, but please remember that you have Vic and me there to handle things. You don't have to bother about the company if you don't want to."

Alice lowered her eyes. There was something about Willis—the way his mouth lifted at the corner when he smiled and the tone of his voice —that reminded her of Steven. He brought up all sorts of emotions in her, emotions she didn't especially want to deal with. The resemblance also made it very hard to get even a little angry at Willis. Nevertheless, she thought it was important to be firm. "I'm glad you and Vic are there, but I may want to 'bother about the company,' as you put it. But, as I told you, I haven't decided yet."

The waiter brought the coffee and poured it from an elegant silver pot. Then he passed them the dessert menus. "Would you care for something else?" Willis asked politely.

She scanned the menu. "I don't think so."

"I guess I'll have the cherry pie," he said, handing his menu back to the waiter. "And could you bring it right away?" he asked, glancing at his watch. "We're in a little bit of a rush."

The waiter nodded before hurrying over to the dessert trolley and bringing back the pie.

"I'm glad you could join me for lunch," Alice said. "I know this is taking you away from the site."

"No problem," he answered smoothly, swallowing a bite of his dessert. "Things are going very well out there. They hardly need me."

Alice was surprised. This wasn't the news she expected. "Really? I thought there were some problems with the shopping center."

He gave her a sharp look. "What kind of problems?"

"Budget problems," she said, starting in.

"Did Vic tell you that?" he asked angrily.

Vic was certainly right about Willis's reaction, Alice thought. She was relieved to be able to say, "No, he didn't."

"Then who did?"

"I heard it . . . somewhere else," she said hesitantly. It would be demeaning if she told him that her father had been checking up on him. Better to keep the source of her information vague, she decided.

Willis was silent while the waiter appeared to refill their coffee cups. The moment he was gone, however, Willis took up the conversation. "I think I should know who's spreading these vicious lies, Alice."

"Vicious is a little strong, don't you think?"

"I don't think so. Not when I can promise you that there are absolutely no money problems with the shopping center. Frame Construction will not have to pay one penny in overruns," he said, his voice rising a little.

She didn't know what to say. She had expected apologies, maybe even anger, but not a complete denial. Surely her father couldn't have gotten his figures that jumbled. He never would have called her unless he knew there was a serious problem. She decided to press the matter a little further. "The projections were all correct then?"

Willis sidestepped the question. "Everything is proceeding according to plan." *That's the truth,* Willis thought, sipping his coffee. Carol had deposited a small fortune in the account that was set up for the shopping center. It would simply seem as though the money for the project had come in late from another account, and no one would be the wiser.

"Well, I'm glad to hear that," Alice said smoothly although she was utterly baffled. "We couldn't afford the kind of overruns I was hearing about."

"I just hope that the next time someone comes

to you with silly gossip, you'll discuss it with me before getting all upset."

"I didn't mean to offend you," she put in quickly, more upset than ever.

"No, I understand. In the corporate world, it's easy to make enemies, and obviously I've done just that. That's why you should think twice about coming back to work. It can be rough out there," he said, signaling to the waiter for the check.

"No, this is my treat. After all, I asked you out."

"Don't be silly," he said, pulling out his wallet, as the waiter laid the check beside his coffee cup. "I wouldn't think of letting a beautiful lady pay for her own lunch." He looked deeply into her eyes and smiled.

If she concentrated very hard, she could pretend, if only for a moment, that she was smiling back at Steve.

When Willis arrived at the office about a half hour later, the first thing he did was stop at the reception desk, where Sharlene was fielding calls. "Get into my office," he hissed.

Sharlene put one hand over the mouthpiece of the phone. "Willis, I'm talking to someone."

"The minute—no, the second—you're done, get Joanie out here to cover and come into my office." He stomped off, with Sharlene's wondering eyes following him.

Slamming the door to his office closed, he loosened the tie he had been forced to wear to lunch and shrugged out of his sports jacket. He had been thinking about Alice's disclosure concerning the overruns all the way back from the restaurant, and there was only one person who could have ratted on him: Sharlene.

He'd wanted to believe it was Vic, because that would have just added fuel to the fire of his hatred of the man. But Alice had practically sworn it wasn't Vic, and she wasn't the sort of woman who would lie.

For a short while, he thought Carol might have been the one who talked to Alice. Perhaps she was trying to double-cross him and blame the overruns on him. Maybe she was angry about having to fork over the money. But that was silly, he quickly concluded; Carol couldn't incriminate him without getting herself into trouble. Besides, she was crazy about him. She'd never risk their relationship.

So, with everyone else eliminated, there was only one person left. The most obvious one, really. Someone he had never gotten along with. Willis's thoughts were interrupted by a knock at the door. "Come in, Sharlene."

"Now, what's so important you had to drag me away from my work?" she snapped, annoying him the way only an older sister could.

"Sit down," he said, pointing to an armless wooden chair.

"I'll stand, thanks. Look, I have a million things to do."

"Sit down," he repeated in a tone that could not be argued with.

Sharlene obeyed reluctantly. "All right, what is it?"

"You think you're pretty smart, don't you?" he asked coldly.

"What? What are you talking about?"

Willis crossed his arms. "You knew about the cost overruns on the shopping center project, didn't you?"

A guilty look passed quickly over her face. "Maybe."

"Don't tell me maybe," Willis bellowed, his voice shaking with anger. "How did you find out?"

"I didn't know anything for sure. I just put two and two together after I typed some memos for Carol."

"And then you ran and told Alice about it."

"No," she denied, genuinely surprised. "I never mentioned it to Alice."

Roughly cupping his sister's chin in his hand, he spat, "I don't believe you."

Sharlene jerked her head away. "I don't care if you believe me or not. I told you the truth."

"Is that so? You go home to that big house every night, and you and Alice just sit around having milk and cookies and trading recipes, is that it?"

Standing up, Sharlene said, "Willis, you always were a little worm."

He shot her a look of deadly anger. "A worm, huh? What about you? You were something a lot worse than a worm. Now sit down."

Sharlene sank back down into her chair. *He knows*, she said to herself. *It's not possible, is it? How could he know?*

"So you say you didn't tell Alice about the overruns?"

"No . . . I didn't," she said, finally finding her voice.

"I don't believe you," he snarled, "but I'll leave it for now. You'd better understand, though, that you'll have to play ball my way or you'll be sorry."

She hated the way her brother talked in circles sometimes. "Stop threatening me. If you have something to say, then just come out with it."

He moved over to his desk and sat down. "This is neither the time nor the place. Besides," he added in a scathing tone, "when we have our talk about what a great gal you are, I may want Russ to be there."

"Russ?" she asked, now wildly upset, but trying to hide it. "What does this have to do with Russ?"

"You never know," Willis replied with an evil little grin. "However, if you want to stay in my good graces, you'll do what I want."

"Which is?"

"Alice is thinking of coming to work here," Willis started to explain.

"I didn't know that," Sharlene broke in, surprised.

"Oh, then Alice doesn't confide in you the way you do in her?" he observed mildly. "Anyway, I don't think having Alice in the office is a very good idea."

"Why not, it's her company."

For now, he amended silently. "Nevertheless, I want you to do everything you can to make Alice change her mind about this plan of hers."

Sharlene shook her head. "I don't have that kind of influence over Alice. We're really not even very close friends. She only took me in because I was Steve's sister and I needed a place to stay."

"So you just sleep under the same roof?" he quizzed.

"Basically, yes."

"Then you'll have to change that," Willis ordered. "I want you and Alice to become very good friends."

"What's going on? I don't understand any of this."

"You don't have to understand it. All you have to know is that if you ever try to cross me again, or if you can't change Alice's mind about coming to work, you're in big trouble."

Rising out of her chair, Sharlene walked toward the door. "You can't threaten me," she said boldly. "You'd better not touch me."

"Be serious, will you? You act as though I'm going to hit you or something. Well, I wouldn't. But I can talk, and my words could hurt you more than any beating would." Willis let out a mirthless laugh.

With his laughter ringing in her ears, she bolted from her brother's office and slammed the door behind her. For a moment she just leaned against the wall, shaking. He had to know. What else could he be referring to? *No*, she thought, trying to calm herself, *there is no way he can know*. Still, for the rest of the afternoon, Sharlene did her work with an icy chill around her heart.

It was almost five o'clock when she went into the ladies' room to freshen up for her date with Russ, who was going to pick her up outside in just minutes. Carol was standing at the full-length mirror, applying a shade of bright pink lipstick that looked terrific with her fair coloring and green eyes.

"Hi, Sharlene," she greeted cheerily, snapping her lipstick case closed. "Long day, huh?"

Sharlene looked at her co-worker closely, trying to see if she was on Willis's side in his effort to upset her. She didn't seem to be, but Sharlene wasn't sure. Carol's expression certainly was open and friendly. "Yes," she finally replied, "it's been a very long day."

Carol watched as Willis's sister splashed some water on her face. "That's a pretty dress. Doing something special tonight?"

Smoothing down the yellow silk sheath she had worn for her date, Sharlene smiled. The dress had seemed perfect when she'd tried it on that morning, but with all of her brother's threats and insinuations, Sharlene felt as if she'd been through a storm. "I'm not sure what Russ has planned. We'll go out to dinner, I suppose."

She looked at Sharlene curiously. "For someone who has a date with a handsome, successful cardiologist like Russ Matthews, you don't seem very happy."

"Oh, no, I'm happy." Then, deflecting the conversation away from herself, she asked Carol, "What about you? Are you happy with the way your relationship with Willis is going?"

Carol actually blushed. No one was supposed to know that she and Willis were an item, but it was hard to hide that kind of thing in a small office. She certainly didn't see any harm in talking to Sharlene about it. After all, she was his sister, and if things turned out the way Carol hoped, someday they'd be family. "Well, Willis thinks it's a good idea to be discreet, but, yes, I'm thrilled he and I are dating. He's wonderful, so take-charge." Carol let out a little laugh. "But I don't have to tell you. I'm sure you know all about Willis."

"I certainly do." Sharlene wanted to add that he also used people and could be dangerous, but there was no easy way to say it. If she meddled in her brother's romantic affairs, he would really be furious. And after his terrible display earlier, she was sure he'd exact some terrible revenge. So instead, she gave Carol a noncommittal smile and said, "I hope it all works out." Then she changed the subject to office matters, and freshened her makeup while she and Carol idly chatted. After leaving the bathroom, Sharlene went to her desk and gathered a few things before hurrying outside to meet Russ.

Her heart always leaped a little when she saw Russ waiting for her. He was so handsome; a tall, broad-shouldered man with a confidence that radiated from him. That must come from being a surgeon, she thought. She certainly never noticed that sureness in the men back home in Chadwell, Oklahoma.

Russ's eyes lit up when he saw Sharlene approaching. "Hi, there," he said as she got into the car. He gave her a little kiss. "You look terrific."

All thoughts of her brother and his threats seemed to magically disappear, and Sharlene and Russ had a beautiful evening dining and dancing at Tall Boys.

But as the evening drew to a close, Sharlene grew pensive, once more thinking about Willis's words. Russ was holding her tight during the band's most romantic song, but he could tell she wasn't really with him.

"Hey," he said, pulling back and looking deep into her brown eyes, "a penny for your thoughts."

"I'm not sure they're worth a penny," she replied, smiling ruefully.

"You look worried, and that's hardly the kind of expression I should see on my lovely lady's face. Won't you tell me what's wrong?"

She would have loved to spill out everything that had happened, but that would be a mistake. Russ might say something to Alice, and if in turn Willis found out, he'd be furious. Besides, she wasn't sure yet what his threats meant. Maybe he knew something he could use to ruin her relationship with Russ. No, there wasn't any way she could safely confide in Russ.

Trying to paste a bright smile on her face, she said, "There's nothing wrong. How could there be? I'm with you, aren't I?"

He held her close as they swayed silently to the music. Then he whispered in her ear, "Just remember, I'm always here for you, no matter what."

Sharlene buried her face in his broad shoulder. *No matter what*, she thought. *Oh, Russ, if only I could believe that.* She brushed away the small tear that slid silently down her cheek.

Soaps & Serials™ Fans!

★ Order the *Soaps & Serials*™ books you have missed in this series.

★ Collect other *Soaps & Serials*™ series from their very beginnings.

★ Give *Soaps & Serials*™ series as gifts to other fans.

...see other side for ordering information

You can now order previous titles
of *Soaps & Serials*™ Books by Mail!

Just complete the order form, detach, and send together
with your check or money order payable to:

Soaps & Serials™
120 Brighton Road, Box 5201, Clifton, NJ 07015-5201

Please circle the book #'s you wish to order:

(A) The Young and The Restless	1 2 3 4 5 6 7 8 9 10 11
(B) Days of Our Lives	1 2 3 4 5 6 7 8 9 10 11
(C) Guiding Light	1 2 3 4 5 6 7 8 9 10 11
(D) Another World	1 2 3 4 5 6 7 8 9 10 11
(E) As The World Turns	1 2 3 4 5 6 7 8 9 10 11
(F) Dallas™	1 2 3 4 5 6 7 8 9 10 11
(G) Knots Landing™	1 2 3 4 5 6 7 8 9 10 11

Each book is $2.50 ($3.50 in Canada).
Total number of books
circled_____ × price above = $ _____

Sales tax (CT and NY residents only) $ _____

Shipping and Handling $ _____.95

Total payment enclosed $ _____
(check or money orders only)

Name_____

Address _____ Apt# _____

City _____ State _____ Zip _____

Telephone (____)_____
          AREA CODE

AW 11

Chapter Seven
Meetings

When Steve had built Alice's dream house, he had made sure it was beautifully suited for entertaining. The spacious, wood-beamed living room was designed to lead into the graciously appointed dining room, and from there French doors opened onto a landscaped garden.

Since Steve's death, however, there hadn't been many parties. But Alice had decided it would be nice to start entertaining again on a small scale. Ray Gordon's return to Bay City seemed like a good excuse for a family dinner, so she had invited her father, Russ and Sharlene, and of course Sally and Beatrice for what she hoped would be a special evening. Pat and the twins had been issued an invitation as well, but Michael was busy and neither Pat nor Marianne was up to coming.

The weather the night of the party was unusually balmy, and Alice had opened the French doors, allowing a soft, spring breeze to waft in from the garden. She had spent the day rushing around with last-minute preparations, but now she was finishing up her final task: arranging yellow and white tulips in a crystal vase.

As she fussed with the lovely flowers, her thoughts turned to Ray. Their relationship certainly hadn't gotten off to a very good start, she thought, but they had parted friends.

Ray's mother had asked him to come to Bay City when she'd discovered that Sally was her granddaughter. Since Ray was a lawyer, Beatrice had wanted him to help her get custody of the child. But he'd had his own ideas about that; he wanted Sally to be raised in California with his family. Eventually, however, he had given in to his mother's wishes and dropped his own plans to gain custody of his niece.

Despite the fact that they were on opposite sides of a legal battle, Alice had always found Ray to be an honest, fair person. After he left Bay City, he had phoned her a few times to check up on Sally, and Alice was surprised to realize that she looked forward to those calls. And now that he was coming back to Bay City to live, Alice wanted him to feel welcome.

As she turned away from her flowers, Alice caught a glimpse of herself in the gilt-framed mirror hanging over the sideboard. She had gone through so much since Steve's death. Did she look any different? she wondered. She examined her reflection. She was thinner, perhaps, and her expression was much more serious, but basically she looked the same. It was surprising, really. Shouldn't every moment of sadness and grief be etched on her face, just as it was etched on her heart?

Alice absently ran her hand through her blond hair. She was still a young, attractive woman. Her sister, Pat, even asked her every once in a while if she didn't think it was time to start dating again. Alice couldn't quite accept that idea yet. Certainly, there were men she found appealing—Ray Gordon, for one—but go out on a date? No, she wasn't ready.

"Sweetheart, what are you doing just staring into the mirror?"

The spell of her reverie broken, Alice turned away from the mirror and looked into her father's eyes. "Lost in thoughts, I guess," she said, giving him an impulsive kiss.

"Honey, can we talk for a moment before the others arrive?" he asked gently.

She sensed the urgency in his tone, and drew him over to a corner of the dining room. "Of course, Dad. What is it?"

"Well, as you know, I was quite surprised when you told me that Willis denied there were any overruns."

"Did you have time to check the books?" she questioned anxiously.

"Yes, I did, and they balance out. There's even a small surplus."

"How could that be?" Alice asked, puzzled.

"Well," he replied carefully, "obviously a considerable sum of money was deposited after I talked to you."

"Oh," said Alice, her expression clearing, "then everything's all right."

"I don't know."

"But you said the debt was cleared up."

"That's just it," her father explained. "I suppose it's not impossible that a large deposit would be made this far into the construction, but it isn't very likely."

Alice patted her father's shoulder, and started checking the place settings on the dining room table. "Don't worry about it, Dad. It was probably just posted late. Or maybe someone in the office forgot to deposit it."

"That doesn't say much for the efficiency of the office staff," Jim commented grimly.

"I'm just relieved it's all taken care of. Besides, once I start working at Frame, nothing like that will ever happen again," she quipped lightly.

"So you've decided to take your place as the working president of Frame Enterprises."

"Yes, I have." Lines of doubt creased her forehead and she gave her father a questioning look. "You think I'm doing the right thing, don't you?"

Jim put his arm around his daughter's shoulder and kissed her golden hair. "I have every confidence in you, honey. I'm sure you'll do what's best."

The doorbell interrupted their moment together. "Well," Alice said, straightening her pearl necklace, "shall we go see who's here?"

When she looked around the living room an hour later, Alice was pleased to see that everyone seemed to be having a good time. Beatrice's hors d'oeuvres were perfect, and Sally looked so cute as she helped the maid Alice had hired for the evening. Then she noticed her father and Sharlene tucked away in a corner. She hoped he was not bothering Sharlene about the discrepancy in the books for the shopping mall. She was happy that it had all worked out satisfactorily, but she knew her father was not one to let the details of the incident go. Sure enough, when she moved closer she realized that his conversation with Sharlene centered on the surprising deposit of funds.

"So you don't have any idea where the money came from?" he asked, sipping his drink.

"Not really."

"You didn't deposit it then?"

"No, but that's not unusual," she explained. "Willis often handles those kinds of details himself."

"Perhaps I should talk to Willis," he said thoughtfully. "He should have the answers."

Sharlene took a shrimp canapé from the tray the maid was passing. "You seem pretty upset about this, Mr. Matthews."

"Accounting is a very precise occupation. I guess it just bothers me when something doesn't add up, so to speak."

"And this doesn't?" she probed.

"Not in my view, no."

Alice walked over and tucked her arm through Sharlene's. "Dad, you're not talking business, are you?"

"Guilty, I'm afraid," he answered, a bit sheepishly.

"It's all right," Sharlene said quickly. "I admire your father's thoroughness."

"So do I"—Alice directed a smile at her father—"but this evening is supposed to be for pleasure, not work. Let's try to just have fun."

The evening went smoothly after that, but to Alice's disappointment, business matters did come up again when dinner was over and everyone was having their coffee.

"Mom, can I play my piano piece after supper?" Sally asked when she was finished with her dessert.

Alice smiled across the table at her. "Normally, I might say no, but I have a sneaking suspicion that this is one crowd that would love to hear you."

Ray agreed. "I have come three thousand miles and it would be a wasted trip if I didn't get to hear you play 'Jingle Bells.'"

"And 'The Spinning Song,'" Sally prompted him.

"'The Spinning Song,' of course," Ray replied with a laugh.

"Good," Sally said happily. "May I be excused, Mom? I want to look over my music."

"Certainly," Alice answered, trying to suppress a grin. "I think that's what all the concert pianists do before a big engagement."

As soon as Sally was out of the room, Beatrice let out a heavy sigh. "I swear, Alice, that little girl is so sweet. I don't see how you can go back to work and leave her."

An uneasy hush fell over the table, and Russ diplomatically tried to smooth things over. "But what better person to help look after her than you, Beatrice."

She appreciated the flattery, but she wasn't about to drop the subject. "Thank you. Sally and I do have a lovely relationship, of course, but it seems to me that when Alice got custody of her, she took on the responsibility of raising her full-time."

Alice looked as though she were about to cry, and Ray also jumped to her defense. "Now, Mother, Sally is in school most of the day, and I'm sure Alice will be able to structure her work time around Sally's schedule. After all, she is the president of the company."

His mother shot Ray a withering glance. "I'm surprised at you. You never allowed Olive to work. Don't the same standards hold for Alice, especially since she's raising your own niece?"

"I didn't force her to stay home, Mother. Olive didn't want to work. Obviously Alice does. Anyway, I think we should drop the subject for now, don't you?"

Beatrice looked around and saw more than a few uncomfortable looks. Naturally, they would think everything dear Alice did was just perfect, she reminded herself. She decided to give in graciously, now that she had spoken her piece. "Certainly. I'm sure Alice will think about it and do the right thing. Let's all go into the living room and listen to Sally, shall we? She's probably waiting for us." With that, the older woman pushed away from the table and headed for the living room, where her granddaughter was practicing noisily.

As the others followed, Ray hung back and waited for Alice, who had taken a moment to compose herself.

"I'm sorry about Mother," he said, sincerely apologetic.

"It's all right. Maybe I should listen to her."

"Oh, you don't mean that," he scoffed.

"I've always been unsure about whether going back to work was the right thing to do," Alice revealed. "If Beatrice feels so strongly about this, maybe I should give it some more thought."

"Give her a while to get used to the idea," Ray counseled. "I think wanting to get involved in Steve's company is admirable, and I'm sure that in a little while, Mother will think so, too."

The next morning, however, while Beatrice did the breakfast dishes, she had plenty of time to reconsider Alice's decision, and she came to the same conclusion all over again. In fact, the more she thought about it, the angrier she became. Her black mood was interrupted by a knock at the door. Wiping her hands on her apron, she opened the door and was surprised to see Willis standing there.

"Hello, Beatrice. Is Alice home? I was passing by and thought I'd drop off these papers."

"No, she's gone out for a while. I thought she might be down at that office of yours," she said sourly.

"You don't sound very happy about her working," Willis observed with interest.

She saw no reason to hide her feelings. "No, I'm not."

"Really? Hey, I'm just dying for a cup of coffee.

You wouldn't happen to have one handy, would you?"

"Don't be silly," she said, recognizing an ally. "I always have a fresh pot of coffee on the stove. Come on in."

Willis made himself comfortable at the round kitchen table while Beatrice poured him some coffee and put a plate of fresh-baked cookies next to his cup. Then she took off her apron and joined him.

"Good cookies," he complimented, taking a bite. "Did you bake them or did Alice?"

"Alice? You're kidding, right? She's been so busy reading and getting ready for this job, we hardly see her."

"And the responsibility for the whole house falls on you?" he prompted, looking suitably sympathetic.

"You bet. Now Sharlene *and* Alice are going to waltz out of here and leave all the messy jobs—" Embarrassed, she caught herself. "Uh, sorry. Sharlene's your sister, isn't she?"

He patted her hand. "Don't worry about it. You know," he began in a confidential tone, "I don't really agree with women working, especially if they don't need the money. Sharlene gets a widow's pension from the Navy, so she doesn't have to work. And Alice . . ." Willis let his voice trail off.

"That's right," she jumped in. "Alice doesn't have to bother herself with work. Besides, she's got Sally to consider."

He shook his head. "I don't know why she doesn't see that."

"Me, either," Beatrice agreed, taking a sip of her coffee.

"I guess it's just the kind of thing you'll have to keep reminding her about."

She shook her head. "Not me. I spoke my mind last night and all I got was a lot of back talk and dirty looks."

"But someone has to show Alice where her responsibilities lie," he argued in his most persuasive tone.

"Do you really think so?" she asked thoughtfully.

"I know so."

It didn't take much to sway Beatrice. She soaked up Willis's words like a wilting flower in the rain. "You know, I think you're right. Even if she doesn't want to hear it, she must be told the truth."

Fixing his gaze on the older woman, he assured her, "You're absolutely correct." He looked very serious, but he was sporting a big smile on the inside. The rougher Beatrice made things at home, the easier things would be for him.

"Well, I've got to be going," he said, taking a final swallow of his coffee. "I guess I'll take these papers to the office. It looks like I'll probably catch Alice there."

"You do that, young man. But let's hope that before long she'll decide to stay home where she belongs."

If some people were worried about Alice spending too much time away from home, others were upset about Marianne Randolph being in the house too much.

Since the evening of her confrontation with her father, she had pretty much stayed in the house, mostly in her room, coming down only every now and then for a light meal. She wouldn't even accept her father's phone calls, and she barely spoke to her mother.

Michael, on the other hand, had a little better luck with her, but not much. At least she would talk to him when he came over. Once in a while, he could even coax a smile from her when he reported some anecdote concerning a mutual friend. For the most part, however, Marianne was listless and unhappy.

Michael spent a good deal of time wondering what to do about his sister's problems. One day, while walking around the Bay State campus, he decided that the time had come to take action. He was going to have to shake her up somehow; anything was better than just allowing her to sit in that dismal room.

Remembering how interested Darrell had been when he'd spoken to him that night in the union, Michael came up with a plan. That night, Darrell had offered to do whatever he could to help. Perhaps the time had come to seek him out.

Even as he started looking for Darrell, he had no clear idea of exactly what he wanted his friend to do. Would Marianne even go out on a date if Darrell asked her, he wondered. Surely she had to be as tired of her behavior as everyone else was. Maybe all she needed to get out of the house was an excuse, which a date with a nice guy would certainly be.

When he caught up with Darrell at the library, they went to the lounge where they could talk. Michael brought him up to date on what was happening with Marianne. Without going into all the messy family details, he told him that his sister was depressed about their parents' separation and badly needed some company, even if she was reluctant to admit it. Darrell quickly agreed to try to cheer her up, even though he understood that it would not be an easy task.

After calling ahead to ask his mother if Marianne was dressed and out of her room, which she was, he and Darrell drove over to the house.

When they came in, they found Marianne idly leafing through a magazine. She looked up with surprise when she saw Darrell standing there. It had been a long time since someone other than a family member had visited her.

"Hi. You remember Darrell Stevens, don't you?" Michael asked, trying to sound casual.

Marianne gazed at the tall, young man with the friendly, open face, and gave him a small smile. "Yes, I remember."

"We were in a math class together," Darrell said, taking a seat near her.

"If I remember right, we both almost flunked that class," she commented.

"That's right." He paused. "Now I'm having some problems with chemistry. I'm a philosophy major and until I get my science requirements out of the way, I guess I'm going to be in for a rough time."

She didn't say anything, so Darrell continued,

just a trace of nervousness in his voice. "Anyway, Michael tells me you're pretty good in chemistry and I was wondering if you might have some time to tutor me."

Startled, she shook her head and said quietly, "I don't think so."

Darrell flashed her a disarming grin. "I would be glad to pay for your time. You see, I already checked at the tutoring office, and no one's available in chem right now. If I don't find someone soon . . ." He lifted his hands and shrugged.

"Come on, Marianne. Help the poor guy out," Michael put in.

"Look, I'd like to help you—"

"Then do," he interrupted.

She tried desperately to think of a reason to say no, but none came to her. She certainly had the time, and Darrell knew she was good in chemistry. Since she was on the spot, Marianne decided to just say yes for now and hope that he would drop the idea after a tutoring session or two. "All right," she said unenthusiastically. "I guess we can give it a try."

Darrell smiled. "That's terrific. Thanks," he said gratefully.

Michael rubbed his hands together. "Okay, when do we get this show on the road."

Marianne shot her brother a dirty look. "You don't mean you want to start the tutoring sessions now."

"Why not? You're both here, and Darrell's got his chemistry book with him. What's standing in your way?"

"It's just that I don't think I'm prepared for it right now," she tried to insist.

"Sure you are," Michael pushed. He took his sister's arm and steered over to the dining room table. Darrell followed behind them and took a seat next to her. "Now, I'll just fix you two something to drink and maybe some chips to keep you going. Just go ahead."

Marianne gave her brother a furious look, but then she turned toward Darrell and resolutely opened the book he handed her. "All right, let's start back at Chapter Three."

Michael and Darrell looked at each other over Marianne's head and smiled.

"You win," John said, pulling off his handball glove. He leaned against the white cement wall for a moment to catch his breath.

Robert came up and clapped him on the shoulder. "Good game, considering you're so out of practice," he teased.

Handball games used to be a weekly event for John and Robert, but as their work loads had increased and their personal problems became more pressing, the games had become monthly. Finally they dwindled to every once in a while.

John rubbed his neck with a towel. "You're out of practice, too. I don't know how you won."

"Chalk it up to my natural ability."

"I'll chalk it up to luck. How about something to drink?"

"Great," Robert said. "Loser buys."

They wandered over to the snack bar, which was

located in the far corner of the health club. John paid for his club soda and Robert's orange juice. Then they moved to one of the booths, where they had a degree of privacy in the midst of the club's bustling surroundings.

"We really have to start doing this more often," John said, taking a sip of his drink. "It's a great way to work all the kinks out."

"Things still bad with Pat?" Robert asked soberly.

He nodded. "Marianne and Michael, too. They're barely civil to me."

"It's not an easy situation," Robert agreed.

"Sometimes I'm just so angry that things went this far. I should have been more protective of my marriage."

Robert fiddled with the straw in his drink. "It's hard to know what to do when a marriage goes off the track."

John detected a note of personal anguish in his friend's voice. Obviously, he was not talking only about John and Pat's relationship. "Are things going sour with you and Iris, too?"

Robert told John that he had finally persuaded Iris to seek professional help, fearing that she was near, if not in the middle of, a nervous breakdown. The words just came tumbling out as he explained about Mac and Iris's fight, about Mac's suspicions of her role in Rachel's miscarriage, and Iris's denial of the whole thing. When he finally finished his monologue, Robert thought his friend seemed a little pale. "Are you all right?"

John was at a loss for words. During Robert's

speech, he'd wondered how much he should tell his friend. Was there any question of lawyer-client confidentiality here? He didn't think so. When Tracey DeWitt had come to him with the information concerning Iris's role in the miscarriage, she'd told him to do whatever he wanted with it. John had gone to Rachel with the truth, and she had obviously told Mac. He couldn't see any real reason why Robert shouldn't know the facts as well.

"Robert, I think I know something that could help you." He then quickly outlined his actions and the reasons for them.

Now it was Robert's turn to blanch. "Then you're sure that Iris didn't give Mac his message from Rachel?"

"Tracey was there, and there's no real reason why she would lie."

Robert gasped. "My God, this means that Iris actually caused the miscarriage. In fact, she could have been responsible for Rachel's death."

John hated to see his friend so upset. He tried to calm him down by saying, "Rachel was already having pains when she called your house. Perhaps nothing could have been done at that point."

"You're defending her?" Robert said, quite shocked.

"No, of course not. She's obviously way too involved in her father's life. But if she had really known how serious Rachel's condition was, I doubt she would have kept it from Mac."

"I wonder," Robert mused bitterly. "I'm not sure I know anything about Iris or her actions."

"So what are you going to do now?"

"About my marriage? Who knows?"

"You're not going to leave Iris, are you?" John asked.

"I don't see how I can. She's on the edge as it is. If I walked out, it would devastate her."

"Well, you can't leave, then," John agreed. "You'd never forgive yourself if something happened."

Robert sighed heavily. "You're right, of course. I'd be no better than Iris if I left her now. But as far as our relationship goes, this is just one more nail in the coffin."

Chapter Eight
Company Business

Sitting in the plush outer offices of Cory Publishing, Pat was leafing through a magazine when she saw Ray walk by. Before she could call out to him, though, he'd turned his head and noticed her.

"Pat," he said, coming over to take her outstretched hand, "how are you?"

"Just fine, thanks. I'm sorry I couldn't join you for dinner at Alice's the other night, but I had a previous engagement." It was a little white lie. Actually, Pat had felt unable to handle an evening out, and she didn't know how to say so without going into all the messy details.

"You missed a lovely evening, but it's certainly good to see you now. What are you doing here?"

Pat looked a little embarrassed. "I'm on a job interview," she admitted.

"Really?"

"As you may already know, John and I are separated. I decided that I needed to get a job, and since Mac's an old friend . . ." Her voice trailed off. "You don't think I'm being too presumptuous, do you? I really don't have much work experience."

"Of course not. Besides, maybe it'll be your lucky day; it was mine. Mac just hired me."

"How wonderful! To do what?"

"I'm going to be heading up the insurance division. They've decided they need an in-house lawyer."

"Does Alice know?"

"I'm just on my way to see her," he said, suddenly looking a little shy.

"She'll be so pleased," Pat assured him. "Is she in the office today?"

"As a matter of fact, she is. She said something about having lunch brought in for us as sort of a christening for her new venture."

"That sounds delightful," Pat replied. "I'm going to have to get over to her office to see it for myself one of these days. Somehow, I just can't picture my baby sister making executive decisions."

The truth of the matter was that even though Alice was sitting in Steven's old office, she couldn't imagine making those decisions, either. She had been coming into the office for more than a week now, but all she'd done was rearrange the furniture. Vic had been very good about showing her the ropes, acquainting her with the various projects and introducing her to the employees, who had been terribly nice. But the fact of the matter was, she still had nothing to do.

By the time Ray arrived for lunch, Alice was really in a blue mood and having serious second thoughts about her decision to head the Frame Enterprises staff.

"Hi," Alice said moodily when he walked into her office.

"That's no way to greet . . . is that a glum face I see?"

She couldn't help smiling. "Maybe."

"Sorry, but glum faces aren't allowed in here, not when I'm walking on air."

"You got a job!" Alice cried with pleasure.

"I got more than *a* job; I got *the* job. You are now looking at the new head of Cory Publishing's insurance division."

Alice got up from behind her desk and offered him her hand. "Congratulations."

He wished she'd thought a kiss on the cheek was appropriate, but obviously she didn't. "Thank you," he said, accepting her good wishes. "Actually, this is the second time today I've shaken hands with one of the Matthews sisters."

"You saw Pat?"

"She was waiting to see Mac while I was over at Cory. Apparently she's job hunting, too."

"Good." She motioned Ray over to the small table the caterers had set up for lunch. "I bet she'll get a job in no time, and a good one, too. Something where she actually has some responsibilities."

He held her chair for her. "What do you mean by that?"

"I'm just a figurehead here, Ray. I should be at home with Sally, and instead I'm coming here every day for no reason," she blurted out.

"I can see you're upset, but it's not really so bad. You don't have to be a figurehead if you don't want to be."

"Maybe, but everyone has a job to do except me. I just sit in this office all day waiting for someone to ask me something. And so far, they haven't."

"Do they have any reason to ask you questions?" he probed gently.

She began serving the cold pasta salad. "Of course not."

"Why do you think that is?"

"Isn't it obvious?" she snapped just a little sharply. "It's because I don't know anything about how the company works."

Ray took a bite of his roll and chewed it thoughtfully. "You're the president of the company, but you have never been directly involved in running it. People aren't going to come to you asking for help unless they think you have something to offer."

Now Alice was becoming quite irritated. Was he just trying to point up her inadequacies? "How do I go about doing that, Mr. Gordon?"

He shrugged. "How did you learn about nursing?"

"I studied and I got experience on the job."

"There you have it. It's up to you to find out everything you can about this business, and then see ways in which you can get involved."

She saw his point, but suddenly she wasn't sure she could do it. "What if I can't manage that?"

"Don't be silly. You're a bright woman, and there's no reason in the world why you can't transfer many of the skills you used as a nursing supervisor to this new position."

Pouring a cup of coffee for herself and one for Ray, she said, "So once I make a contribution, people will naturally seek me out."

"Exactly."

"Perhaps you're right," she conceded. "After all, there isn't much reason for them to come to me now."

Ray smiled at her. "Problem solved, at least in theory."

"That takes care of one, I guess," Alice agreed, "but believe me, I have others."

"You mean about thinking you should be at home with Sally."

She nodded. "It's a very difficult situation."

"You feel guilty, don't you?"

"Yes. I'm sorry to have to say this, but your mother isn't helping."

Ray shook his head. "I expected something like this. What's Mother been saying now?"

"Nothing awful. She just always has some kind of a comment whenever I walk in the door. And when she isn't saying something, she's looking at me as though she's terribly disappointed in the way I've been caring for Sally."

Ray hated to see Alice looking so upset. He was going to have to talk to his mother, but for the moment he tried to keep his voice calm. "How's Sally reacting to your going to work?"

"Just fine. When she comes home from school, I'm already back from work. We usually sit and talk for a while about what we've done that day."

"It sounds like you're doing pretty well to me."

"I am. At least, I think I am until Beatrice starts harping at me."

Ray picked at his food. "Let me tell you a little story. When Jenny and I were young, Mother would breathe down our necks every moment of the day. As bad as it was for me, it was worse for Jenny. Mother practically kept her under lock and key."

"Really?" Alice said, surprised. "From the way she talks about Jenny, I thought they had the ideal mother-daughter relationship."

He let out a bitter laugh. "Don't you believe it for a second. Why do you think Jenny ran away?"

"The relationship was too intense?" she guessed.

"Absolutely."

"You know," she confided, "I was afraid I was getting to be that way with Sally. Once I had custody, I wanted to spend every minute with her; I didn't even like her to visit her friends."

"That's not good for either of you," Ray said, shaking his head.

"I know that now. I think we'll appreciate each other more if we're not always on top of each other."

"You're right. And if I were you, I wouldn't worry about what my mother says and does. Just ignore her. Your only problem will come if you decide you want her out of the house."

"It hasn't come to that yet," Alice said, taken aback.

"Well, it might. To put it bluntly, Mother can get on your nerves. After a little while, you may not think the headaches are worth it."

"I would never want to separate Sally from her grandmother," she replied.

"Their relationship wouldn't have to end if Mom lived and worked somewhere else."

Alice shook her head. "I can't think about that right now. Let's just hope it works out."

"I'll keep my fingers crossed."

"Let's change the subject," she said firmly. "What do you think of my office?"

He looked around. The room was handsomely decorated, with expensive leather chairs and an antique desk. Silver-framed photographs of some of the buildings Frame Construction had worked on were on the walls. "Very impressive," he finally commented. "You have quite a tradition to continue."

"I know. That's another thing I'm worried about."

"Don't be. You're one of the most capable women I know."

And one of the most beautiful, he added silently. Maybe one day he would have the guts to tell her so. He'd tell her that ever since he had first met her in Bay City he hadn't been able to get her out of his mind. And he would tell her that one of the reasons he had been able to finally face the fact that his marriage to Olive was over was because the future held the promise of seeing her.

Oblivious to Ray's inner turmoil, Alice went over to the side table and took a chocolate cake out of its cardboard box. "How does this look?" she asked, holding it up.

"Wonderful," he answered, but the comment was directed more toward Alice than the dessert.

The day had been a long one for Willis. Early that morning he'd had a meeting with Jim Matthews, who was determined to find out where the cash had come from to pay for the overruns on the shopping center. Willis had put on his most charming face, but Jim wanted answers, not smooth talk. Finally, Willis told him the money had been posted to the wrong account and it had taken a while to unscramble the mistake. It didn't make Willis and his staff look very efficient, but it was the best he could come up with on the spot. Jim had dryly suggested he be more careful with his books the next time.

Not two minutes after Jim's departure, Sharlene had come waltzing through his door. His visit had made it obvious that he was the one who told Alice about the cost overruns, and she wanted Willis to finally admit he was wrong for blaming her.

If there was one thing Willis hated to do, it was admit he was wrong, but he had no choice. He grudgingly apologized, but at the same time he warned his sister to keep any opinions she might have about him to herself. He also reminded her that she hadn't done a very good job of keeping Alice out of Frame Construction. That put some fear back into her, he noted with some satisfaction.

Now Willis was stalking around his small office complaining to Carol about Alice's lunch with Ray. "What's she doing in there," he asked with disgust, "having a tea party?"

"Oh, what difference does it make? So Alice is having Ray in for a little catered lunch. Let her have her fun. She doesn't really have anything else to do."

"Yeah, well, I don't like the whole thing," he fumed. "Especially Alice getting so friendly with Ray and Sharlene."

Carol stood up and put her hand on his shoulder. "Baby, please calm down. Why do you care what happens in Alice's personal life?"

"You don't get it, do you?" he asked, shaking off her comforting hand. "The more secure Alice feels, the more they encourage her, the more likely she is to start taking charge here in the office. We've got to keep her off-balance."

"Are you sure that's it?" Carol asked.

"Of course I'm sure."

"Well, I don't know how you think you're going to do it. Alice is not stupid; she'll catch on eventually, and then you'll be out."

"I'm working on it, okay," he countered. "But I'm also worried about Vic."

"I agree with you there—Vic is a problem. He's really very good at what he does."

"There are ways around that," Willis said spitefully. "I have several ideas about how to fix Mr. Hastings, and I'm just about to put them into action."

Before he could explain further, Vic rapped at the door and opened it a crack. "Do you two have a minute?" he asked.

Willis immediately turned into the personable, charming young man he could be when he wanted. He was able to slip into that role as easily as other people changed their clothes. "Come in, Vic. You know, you must be psychic, we were just talking about you."

Vic entered. "Good things, I hope."

Subtly, Willis turned to Carol, who picked up her cue. "Absolutely," she said sincerely. "We were just saying you're one of the best at what you do."

He flashed them a pleased grin. "This is turning out to be a very nice day all the way around."

"What's going on?" Carol asked, suddenly curious. "You look like the proverbial cat who ate the canary."

"Very good news for Frame Construction," Vic said proudly. "Lowell Pendleton has just commissioned us to do a three-hundred-unit retirement center outside of Washington, D.C."

Even Willis was impressed. "That sounds like a very big job."

"It is. In addition to the apartments and town houses, there will be a recreation center, a small shopping mall and several other all-purpose buildings."

"I didn't even know we were in the running for a job of that magnitude," Carol commented.

"Pendleton wasn't really interested in taking bids. He knew us by reputation, of course, and then I had several meetings with him. When we spoke the last time, he just about promised that the project was ours, but I didn't want to say anything until it was in writing. I got the letter today."

Willis forced a smile. "Congratulations! Does Alice know?"

"I stopped into her office, but apparently she and Ray went out for a walk."

"She'll be very excited," Carol said with a nervous glance in Willis's direction. She knew he must be seething inside.

"She certainly will be," Vic said, "and so will Robert when I talk to him."

"Robert?" Willis asked, frowning.

"Of course. On a project this big, we'll want Robert to be the architect." Vic looked over toward Carol, just a shade embarrassed. "It is a very complex project. Besides, there's plenty of in-house work to keep you busy."

"Oh, I understand," she assured him quickly. "With something like this, it's no wonder that you'd want Robert's expertise."

"I knew you'd understand." Vic gave Carol a smile. "Well, I'm going to see if Alice is back. I just wanted to give you two the good news."

With a little wave, he left the office. As soon as he shut the door, Willis picked up a heavy folder of papers and threw it across the room.

"Willis!" Carol cried, shocked.

"The nerve of that guy, coming in here gloating about his big new project."

"I don't think it was like that," she said, trying to calm him down.

He turned toward her angrily. "Really? I think it was exactly like that. And what was that humble act you put on? How come you were so nice and polite about Vic giving Robert your job?"

"It was no act. Vic's right, I don't have that kind of experience."

"You could do it," Willis insisted.

"At this point, the question is moot. Vic is going to hire Robert, and he's making a very good decision."

"Are you turning on me?" he asked menacingly.

Carol sighed. "Come on, Willis, you know I'm on your side." She got up and walked to the door. "Let's just try to be happy the company got such an interesting project. I'm sure we'll both be involved, so I don't see why we have to fight with Vic about everything."

After Carol left, he stared off into space. She was right about one thing; they *were* going to be involved with this project. But, it was going to be far more than either she or Vic anticipated. As a matter of fact, there were a couple of things Willis had been meaning to do to get his plans for taking over the company underway, and today was as good a time as any to start them. The first thing he had to do was make a call to Lowell Pendleton.

Pendleton was not in and it took several hours for him to return Willis's call. He phoned just as the office was closing, and Willis was happy that no one was around. This wasn't a conversation he wanted anyone to overhear.

"Mr. Frame, this is Lowell Pendleton," said the voice on the phone. "I'm sorry it took me so long to get back to you, but I've been out all day."

"I understand. Actually, I'm calling for Vic Hastings. He's going to be in and out of the office and he wanted me to introduce myself since you'll be dealing with me quite a bit on our new project."

"Say, are you related to Steve Frame?" Pendleton asked.

"Yes, he was my brother."

"I was a great admirer of Steve's, and it will be a pleasure having a Frame in on this project. I look forward to working with you.

Willis smiled. This was just the sort of reception he had hoped to get. "Thank you, Mr. Pendleton. Now, if you have a moment, there is one thing I'd like to speak to you about right now. I know that Vic mentioned using Robert Delaney on this job, but now we find he may be tied up."

"Really? I'm sorry to hear that."

"It won't be a problem, however, because we have a terrific architect working right here. Her name is Carol Lamonte, and she's quite talented."

Even Carol might not have recognized herself from Willis's glowing description to Lowell Pendleton over the next fifteen minutes. By the end of the conversation, Pendleton had admitted that he was very impressed by what he was hearing and would not be averse to bringing Miss Lamonte in as the architect.

With the suggestion that Pendleton communicate directly with him in the future, Willis said good-bye, satisfied with what he considered a very successful phone call.

Now, he thought, it's time to take care of Vic. Wandering out to the front desk, where Sharlene had been doing some typing earlier in the day, he found just what he was looking for.

There was a letter on Frame Construction stationery waiting for Vic's signature that included the bid for a project near and dear to his heart. It was a relatively small project, but a prestigious one: the renovation of the Bay City Town Hall.

The white stone building was architecturally significant, having been built in the late 1800s. In the thirties, a famous architect of the day had done some work on the interior, but now the entire building needed to be modernized. Both Vic and Alice were very excited about the chance of putting their own imprint on such an important part of the Midwest's history. Willis had overheard Alice saying that this was just the kind of project she would love to be involved with.

Carefully checking the figures, he saw that Vic had estimated the project's cost at $150,000. Willis sat down at Sharlene's desk and retyped the bid, changing the price to $450,000.

That should make sure we lose the project, he thought with satisfaction. Not only would there be no special little project for Alice to get involved with, she would be furious with Vic because of the overbid.

To cover his tracks, he pulled out the original memo. Using the same kind of black pen Vic had used, Willis adjusted the memo, easily transforming the first numeral into a four. If anyone checked, it would seem as though the mistake had been made originally by Vic.

Whistling a cheery little tune, he then filed the original memo, destroyed the copy Sharlene had typed, and signed Vic's name to the new letter. He tucked it into the envelope Sharlene had prepared and put it into his pocket to mail on the way home. With all of that out of the way, Willis made sure the lights were off and the door was locked. As he left the office, he congratulated himself on a good day's work.

Chapter Nine
Lunch at Tall Boys

Pat stood impatiently inside the lobby of Tall Boys, one of Bay City's finest restaurants, waiting for Alice to show up for their luncheon date.

Even though she had been to restaurants all over the United States and Europe, she could never come to Tall Boys without thinking what an elegant place it was. Shimmering chandeliers softly lighted the dining area, and the pale pink and gray decor was stylish and soothing at the same time. It made the waiting easier, though not much.

The Matthews sisters had decided it had been too long since the two of them last sat down for a gossipy chat, so they agreed to meet for lunch and catch up on each other's lives. But Alice should have been there at least half an hour ago, and Pat was afraid that if she was delayed any longer, they would lose their table.

She was just about to give up and leave when Alice appeared, breathlessly pulling off her trench-coat as she entered the restaurant.

"I'm so sorry," she said as the hostess led them to their table. "There was a crisis at work, and I just couldn't get away."

"That's all right," Pat said, her annoyance fading away. "I should have expected it, what with having a lady executive for a dining companion. What was the trouble?"

"I'll tell you after we order," Alice said, scanning the menu the hostess had handed her. "It's really very upsetting."

After making their selections—poached salmon for Pat and linguini for Alice—Alice launched into her story.

"I think I mentioned to you that Frame Construction was up for the renovation of City Hall."

"I do remember you telling me about that. You were very excited."

"I was. It was going to be the first project I co-managed with Vic, and because of the building's history, I was especially interested in it."

"And," Pat prompted.

"Well, Vic assured me we would get the project. He even told me that he underbid a little because he wanted to make sure we would get it. He said whatever we lost, we would make up in prestige."

"I know you've been pretty bored over there, up till now."

"That's for sure. There's been nothing for me to do, so just the thought of getting this has kept me going. I really wanted to do it as a first project because it seemed so much more inspiring than just working on another shopping center or something."

"So, what happened?"

"The letter came this morning; we didn't get it."

Pat was shocked. "You didn't? Why?"

Alice shrugged helplessly. "I don't know. Vic is out of town, but I was able to find out the winning bid because the city government has to post that kind of information."

"How close was your bid?"

"We were way out of line, Pat. About $250,000 off."

"You're kidding!"

"I wish I were," Alice said, getting upset all over again.

"What could have gone wrong?"

"I don't know. Either Vic made a terrible mistake in his calculations, or he just didn't want us to get the job for some reason."

"Could someone have typed up the amount of the bid incorrectly?" Pat asked, trying to come up with an excuse for the discrepancy.

"I thought about that, but I went back to the original bid and it said $450,000 in Vic's handwriting."

"Well, I certainly don't think Vic would do something to deliberately undermine you," Pat said doubtfully.

"I wouldn't have thought so either, but some very strange things have been going on between Vic and me."

Alice paused while the waitress brought them their lunch, but the moment the food had been served, she continued her story. "For one thing, ages ago I wrote Vic a long memo about the direction I wanted the company to take. I kept waiting for him to talk to me about it, but he never has. It's as though he didn't feel it was worthy of comment."

"That doesn't sound like Vic," Pat said.

"No, it doesn't. But there is something else. He's promised dozens of times to send me copies of all his major correspondence, and I haven't gotten those either."

"Have you tried talking to him about this?"

"He's been out of town a lot, but every time I mention that I'm not getting any copies, he says that he's been sending them, so I should be receiving them."

"And you think he's lying."

"The office isn't that big. How could copies of letters just disappear?"

"You're right about that," Pat agreed. "Once or twice, maybe, but not on a regular basis."

"What's worse, if he says he's sending them, I just can't call him a liar."

"What about your memo on the company's future. Did you ever come right out and ask him what he thought about it?"

Alice swallowed a bite of linguini and shook her head. "I couldn't. I was too embarrassed. It seemed like he was just ignoring me."

"You have to talk to him, you know."

"When he gets back into town, I will. But it won't be easy."

Pat could see how uncomfortable her sister was in her new role as boss. She tried to be reassuring.

"I know this is rough on you, but remember that it takes time to step into a position like this."

"I know. I'm trying not to get discouraged, but right now the only bright spot at work is Willis."

"Willis?" Pat asked with surprise.

"Yes, he's doing a wonderful job. He always takes the time to tell me what's going on and explain how I can get involved, too."

"That's nice," Pat said noncommittally.

Alice looked at her curiously. "You don't like Willis, do you?"

"I wouldn't say that, exactly," she answered, concentrating very hard on her meal and not meeting her sister's eyes.

"What would you say—exactly?" Alice persisted.

"I'm not sure I trust him, that's all."

"You felt that way about Steve, too," she said defensively. "You and Mom both disliked him."

"Come on," Pat said with authority in her voice, "we're not going to sit here and argue about the Frame family. Let's change the subject, shall we?"

Alice relaxed a little and her face lost its tense sharpness. "You're right. We can't go back and change things now. There is one member of the Frame family I do want to talk about, though."

"Sharlene?" Pat guessed.

"Yes, I think she and Russ are becoming very serious."

"I've had the same feeling myself," Pat agreed with interest. "Are they really seeing a lot of each other?"

"Oh, yes. They're together almost every evening these days. I see much more of Sharlene at work than I do at home."

"I think it's good for both of them," Pat said emphatically. "After all, they've both had such tragedy in their lives. And, of course, Russ has Rachel in his past." She smiled. "Thank God for Mac Cory; he's really turned Rachel's life around.

"Speaking of Mac," Alice commented, changing the subject, "what have you heard about a job at Cory? It's been several weeks since you interviewed there, hasn't it?"

"Yes," Pat sighed. "I've spoken to Mac a couple of times on the phone, and he's been very nice. He tells me he's waiting for a position to open up and that he's also talked to several other people around Bay City for me, but so far nothing's turned up."

"I'm sure something will soon," Alice said sincerely.

"It'd better be soon," Pat answered, grim-faced. "I'm getting very tired just sitting around the house or doing volunteer work. And you know when I'm bored, my thoughts always turn to taking a drink."

"Pat, no!" Alice cried with alarm. "Maybe I could find some work for you at Frame."

"No, that's all right. Really, I'm fine. And I don't think your company needs two Matthews sisters under one roof. Something else will turn up for me. I just hope it's soon."

"Are you still seeing Dave?" Alice asked cautiously. She knew her sister rarely talked about her friendship with Dr. Gilchrist.

"Sort of. He's been a very good friend."

"How does Marianne feel about him? Is she still having trouble dealing with your separation from John?"

Pat fiddled with her fork. "I don't know what Marianne is thinking these days. She barely talks to me and I know she hasn't spoken to John. He phones the house all the time, but she never takes his calls."

"You're not trying to keep them apart, are you?" Alice asked. She knew her sister's feelings toward John weren't exactly friendly.

"Me? Heavens, no. John has done some terrible things, but I really don't want to see Marianne become estranged from her father. It wouldn't be good for either one of them."

"What does she do all day? She's not taking classes anymore, is she?"

"No. She dropped them all. Mostly, she stays in her room. Once in a while, a friend of Michael's comes over and she tutors him in chemistry."

"That sounds encouraging."

"I guess so. She seems to be doing it out of a sense of duty, though. She barely looks at Darrell when they're together."

"What's this Darrell like? Is he nice?"

"He seems to be. He's quiet, polite, attractive in a studious sort of way."

"Is he tall and thin, with horn-rimmed glasses?" Alice inquired.

"Yes, that's him. Do you know him?"

Alice tilted her head toward the back of the

restaurant. "Don't look now, but coming down the aisle over there is Marianne with Darrell."

Pat cautiously looked over her shoulder, trying to catch the couple out of the corner of her eye. "I don't believe this. This is the first time in weeks I've seen her dressed up, much less out of the house."

Alice turned to get a better look at the duo as they left the restaurant. "I don't know, Pat. She looks pretty happy to me. Maybe your problems are over."

Marianne noticed her mother and aunt just as she and Darrell had been served their desserts, and it almost ruined her ice cream. She was sure they would see her when she left the restaurant, and that angered her. Marianne didn't like the idea of them knowing she was out in public. She preferred to have her mother think she was sitting miserably at home; it gave her a perverse satisfaction.

Darrell noticed immediately when Marianne became uneasy at the table and he asked her about it.

"Is your dessert all right?"

"Why?" she asked sharply.

"Nothing. You look upset all of a sudden."

Darrell had such a worried expression on his face that Marianne softened. "I'm okay."

"I'm glad," he said, relieved. "After all, this is your big day out. I wouldn't want it ruined."

"You know," she said thoughtfully, "it was very nice of you to plan this day for me."

"It's not over yet. Don't forget we're going to the art museum after lunch."

"I'm really looking forward to it. I haven't been to the museum in months."

"Can I ask you a question, Marianne?" Darrell asked, dipping into his ice cream.

"Certainly," she replied.

"What made you decide to come out with me today? Michael says you haven't been anywhere in weeks."

"That's true," Marianne said slowly. "I'm not sure myself why I decided to come." She looked at him for a long moment and then said, as surprised at the answer as he was, "I guess I trust you."

The rest of their lunch passed quickly, and after he paid the bill and escorted her outside into the gleaming sunshine, Darrell said, "Did I just see your mother in there?"

"Yes," Marianne answered curtly.

Darrell was perplexed. "Then why didn't you go over and say hello to her?"

"I just didn't feel like it." She hesitated. "Do you think she saw us?"

"I don't know," he answered, thinking as he had so many times in recent weeks that he really didn't understand Marianne at all.

He led her over to his car, which was parked at the back of the lot, and within a few moments they were out on the highway heading toward the Bay City Art Museum. Although it was small, the museum housed a particularly good collection of American art.

Marianne and Darrell spent two pleasant hours admiring the Wyeths and Pollocks, and when they finally decided to rest their feet, they went out the enclosed glass patio that contained buttery soft leather couches and artwork by students from Bay State's art department. It was deserted at that time of the day, but even so, they tucked themselves away in a corner where their privacy was complete.

"Marianne," Darrell said after they'd settled themselves, "you said earlier that you trusted me."

She flashed him a small smile. "You're not going to blackmail me with that statement, are you?"

"No," he said, his tone serious, "but if you do trust me, I wish you'd tell me what's going on."

She looked away. "I don't know what you mean."

Gently, he cupped her chin and turned her face back toward him. "I think you do. You're miserable, aren't you? You barely speak to your mother and you never go out. Obviously, there is a problem in your life and I wish you would share it with me. I'd like to help."

"You mean Michael hasn't told you the whole story?"

He let out a short laugh. "Hardly. Oh, I've tried to get it out of him often enough, and he's told me a few generalities, but he always says you'll tell me when you're ready." He looked deeply into her eyes. "Are you ready?"

Something inside of her broke. She had spent so many weeks nursing her hurt and anger, and there had been precious few opportunities to release those emotions. Now, with Darrell looking at her so expectantly, it seemed like the right moment to let them go.

He did not even try to interrupt her. Instead, he just let her talk about her disastrous love affair, her pregnancy and subsequent abortion, and the guilt that followed. She also told him about how her problems had caused a rift between her parents and about her shock and anger at discovering that her father had had an affair. Finally, running out of words, she stopped talking. Still, she couldn't stop the tears that ran down her cheeks.

Darrell put a strong arm around her shoulder. "It's all right," he murmured. He took a handkerchief from the pocket of the suit he had worn especially for the occasion, and gently wiped the tears from her eyes.

Marianne took the cloth from him and dabbed at her cheeks. "You must think I'm an idiot."

"Hardly."

"What do you think, then?" she asked softly. "I'd like to know."

"I think you are a wonderful person who has been hurt very deeply. I also think you're irrationally trying to hurt other people in return, and it isn't doing you any good."

Marianne's famous temper flared briefly. "I suppose you think I should just go apologize to everyone and that will be the end of the whole thing."

He didn't try to stop her outburst. Instead, he stared into space. "Marianne, can I tell you a story?"

It was not the reaction she'd expected, but she said, "I suppose so."

"I could say it's about a boy and his father, but the truth of the matter is that it's about me and my own dad."

"Go ahead. Please."

"My dad was a lawyer like yours is, and from the time I was a little kid, I knew I was expected to be a lawyer, too. At first, I thought that was just fine. After all, what kid doesn't want to follow in his father's footsteps when he grows up? But the older I got, the more I realized that the law wasn't for me. I don't have the mind for it, and I don't have the drive. I like art and writing. The law left me cold."

"Kind of like chemistry," Marianne said, trying to lighten Darrell's somber tone a little.

He gave her a rueful smile. "Exactly like chemistry. Well, I didn't know what to do about my father. I'd change my mind every other day. First I was going to tell him I wasn't heading for law school, then I would decide to wait. One day the decision was taken out of my hands. My father sat down with me and went over the classes I'd chosen one by one. It was pretty apparent that I wasn't planning to go into law. Finally, I just flat out told him that."

"What happened?"

Darrell shook his head at the memory. "We had a terrible fight, just awful. We brought up every ugly thing we could think of from the past, and we argued about those, too. I stomped off and refused to speak to him for weeks. My mother tried to patch things up, and then I got mad at her."

"Are you still fighting with your dad?" she asked quietly.

"We can't fight anymore, Marianne. He died about six months ago."

"Oh, no," Marianne said, shocked.

"It's funny, but a few days before he had his heart attack, I had decided I really wanted to get this mess behind us. I was going to go home for a visit when I had a free weekend and straighten everything out. Mom had told me Dad felt really bad about things, too, so I knew we'd make up. It was just a matter of one of us making the first move. But before I could make the arrangements for a trip, Mom called and told me Dad had been taken to the hospital with chest pains. By the time I got home, he was gone."

Marianne's lips were trembling as she said, "It must have been so terrible."

He nodded. "It was. It still is. Sometimes I wonder if I'll ever get over it."

"You will," Marianne comforted him. "You've got to remember that your dad knew you loved him. Underneath all the anger, he had to know that."

"That's what everyone tells me. Mom says Dad was always sure we'd end our fight someday. But I've got to tell you, it's small satisfaction. I never heard him say he forgave me. I never saw him smile at me again. Sometimes I wake up in the middle of the night, and I realize I've been having the most wonderful dream. In it, Dad and I are walking out in our backyard, and we're talking and laughing and I know everything's all right. Every time I have that dream, for the second just before I'm wide awake, I think it's real. It's a wonderful feeling."

Now it was Marianne's turn to offer comfort. "I'm so sorry," she murmured, taking his hand.

Finally, Darrell pulled himself together. "You must know that I didn't tell you this story just to upset you."

"I know," she said so softly that he could barely hear her.

"It's just that I would hate to have the same thing happen to you. I mean, I'm sure your dad's healthy and everything, but"—he stumbled a little —"you just never know. I guess I'm saying there are some things you can't leave to chance."

Totally drained, Marianne rubbed her eyes. How she would have liked to go home and crawl into bed, but she knew that wasn't possible. "I have to go see him, don't I." It wasn't a question, but a statement.

Darrell didn't say anything for a few seconds. Then he asked, "Are you ready to go?"

She didn't answer right away. Her mind flitted back over all the fights and harsh words, all the disappointments. Yet, she had to admit there were disappointments from her side, as well. Finally, she turned to Darrell and gazed at him steadily. "I'm ready. Will you take me to my father's home?"

Chapter Ten
Bittersweet Moments

Both Marianne and Darrell were silent as they sped across town toward her father's apartment. She tried to rehearse the words she wanted to say to him, but they kept getting tangled up with accusations and hurt feelings. She could only hope that once she and her father were alone together, the right words would come.

For his part, Darrell worried that he had overstepped his bounds. It had not been easy to relive the wrenching time before his father's death, but he had done it. It had been a sincere effort to make Marianne see that patching things up with her father was the only thing to do. Still, he didn't know her all that well. Who was he to imagine that he knew what was right for the Randolph family. What if she let her emotions get out of hand and provoked another fight? What if Mr. Randolph rejected his daughter even if she did make an apology? Suddenly it seemed as though he had gotten himself involved in a very sticky situation. If it didn't work out, Marianne might wind up hating him.

When they were almost there, Darrell felt he just had to say something. "Marianne, I think you're doing the right thing, I really do. But things might not . . ." He let his voice trail off, not knowing what to say.

Marianne, however, understood. "What if it doesn't work out? You know, my father hasn't called in a week or so. I suppose there's a chance he will still be angry with me."

"It is a possibility," he conceded, glad to have his worst fears out in the open.

"I've thought of that; I've thought of all the things that could go wrong."

"You have?"

"Yes, but I know it's a chance I have to take. There's no doubt in my mind that the first step has to come from me."

He swung the car into the littered parking lot. "You're doing the right thing," he said sincerely. "Whatever happens, you'll know you've made the effort."

Marianne pulled down the sun visor and looked into the slightly cracked mirror Darrell had attached there. She ran a comb through her hair and, with a shaking hand, applied a little lipstick.

"Do you want me to wait?" Darrell asked with concern.

"That's all right," she said, facing him and giving him a little smile. "It might be easier if I know I have to go inside and work things out. If you're here waiting, I could be tempted to run away if the going gets rough."

"I hope it won't be rough; I hope he welcomes you back with open arms."

She sighed as she let herself out of the car. "Thanks, but I don't think it's going to be that easy. For either of us."

After he drove away, she walked around the parking lot several times, trying to get her courage up. As usual, she found her father's surroundings depressing, and she began to think once more about his coming home and reuniting with her mother. *It's possible*, she reasoned silently. *After all, no one has been angrier at Dad than I have, and we're going to make up now. At least I hope so.*

Knowing that putting things off wouldn't make them any easier, Marianne resolutely headed for the door of the apartment building. She had seen her father's car in the parking lot, and she knew he would be home. All she had to do was go to his apartment and knock. Why did that simple task seem so hard? Finally, summoning up every bit of her resolve, she took the rickety elevator to his floor and rapped at the door.

Her father opened it almost immediately. Surprise and delight lit up his face. "Marianne! Honey, come in." Although he had seen her weeks before, it seemed more like years to him. Then, fingers of fear began to settle in his heart. What was she doing here? Their last meeting was devastating, but surely she hadn't come here to fight with him again?

Shyly, Marianne said hello and walked over to the window that looked out on the dirty little courtyard. She was there, but she couldn't quite face looking at her father yet.

"Is everything all right?" he asked.

She turned to face him. "I think you know it isn't."

"We have a lot to straighten out, don't we?"

"Yes, and I want to clear things up. But to tell you the truth, I still feel angry. There are so many things I don't understand. Can we talk? Honestly?"

He led her over to the couch. "I think we should."

Taking a deep breath, Marianne began. "Dad, why did you do it?"

"You mean the affair?"

Marianne nodded.

"I've been asking myself the same question, over and over. After all this time, I think I've come up with some answers. This all goes back a long way, honey." John sat down on the couch next to Marianne, but then he stood up and began pacing. "Your mother and I were so happy when we got married; at least, we were at first. I had finally just gotten your mother off from that dreadful murder charge, and our future looked so bright. Then you and Michael came along." John's face softened. "A double blessing. Your mother had a difficult time after her pregnancy, though. Her postpartum depression paved the way for her alcoholism. That's when I had the affair."

"The *first* affair," Marianne stressed coldly.

He nodded miserably. "I doubt if I can explain it very well, but Bernice wanted me and your mother . . . didn't."

She knew she should try to be adult about this, but Marianne wanted to put her hands over her ears and blot out the whole discussion. The thought of her father with any woman besides her mother was almost more than she could bear.

John, however, was so absorbed in his story that he hardly noticed Marianne's distress. He had wanted to explain this to his daughter for a long time. "Eventually, of course, we reconciled, but there were other problems along the way."

"Other women?" she asked, almost afraid to hear the answer.

"No," he replied, unable to meet her eyes. "Not until Barbara." He paused before going on. "You were old enough to remember some of the problems we had. There was that trouble when Steve Frame lied at his divorce trial, and I, as an officer of the court, had to turn him in."

She nodded. "Mother was furious. She said you ruined Aunt Alice's only chance of happiness."

"I did what I had to do," John said, his voice strong for the first time since he began talking. "I wish it hadn't been necessary, but it was. I thought so then, and I still believe it."

"I know, Daddy." It was obvious how much the incident still pained him.

"Anyway, Pat and I patched it up as we always had. There were even some wonderful moments. That Christmas trip to Vail." John's eyes misted over. "You remember that, Marianne, don't you? We went skiing. On Christmas Eve we read the Nativity story by candlelight in our little villa."

"Then we blew out the candles and stuffed one another's stockings with presents. Yes, I remember," she said with a catch in her voice.

"There were plenty of good times like that," he agreed. "It's important you know that."

She was about to ask how the current trouble had started, but she could see her father needed to tell the story in his own way. Nervously, she played with a frayed piece of material on the couch as he continued.

"I don't know how to say this without hurting you, but things started to go badly again when you became pregnant."

Marianne's heart sank. How she'd dreaded hearing just that.

"Your mother kept your secret, and I felt so incredibly excluded. I knew something was going on, but no one would say what. Barbara was a good friend, and eventually it turned into more. When your mother found out, well, she took it very hard," he finished in a rush. He turned at the sound of his daughter's crying. "Oh, baby," he said, kneeling beside her and taking her in his arms, "I'm sorry, so very sorry."

She sobbed quietly for a moment, but then wiped her tears away. "I'm not crying because of your affair. I'm upset because I've realized all over again how much of this is my fault. Mom said that I was partly to blame, but I didn't want to hear it. She was being kind, though. We all would have been happier if it wasn't for me." This discouraging thought brought on a new onslaught of tears.

"Honey, please don't cry. The reason I told you the whole story was to make you see that you're not totally responsible. You have to understand that my problems with your mother go way back."

"But if I hadn't made Mom promise not to tell you I was pregnant—"

"Look, Marianne," he interrupted firmly, "your mother and I are adults, and we've both made some very bad decisions along the way. Your mother decided she would keep your confidence; she shouldn't have done that. And I shouldn't have taken my hurt and anger to another woman. I should have made your mother tell me what was going on."

Marianne looked at her father, who was still kneeling beside her, his hands on her shoulders. She pulled away and went over to the other side of the room. She couldn't bear to say what she had to say without cushioning it with some space.

"Daddy, the reason I wouldn't let Mom tell you was because I was so afraid you wouldn't want anything more to do with me. I thought you would be as ashamed of me as I was." She drew a breath. "Are you ashamed of me?"

Instead of answering her question, he countered with one of his own. "Are you ashamed of me?"

She didn't say anything right away. She thought about her father's behavior and how it had hurt her. She remembered the hours she'd spent crying because her father was not the perfect man she had always thought he was. But was she ashamed of him? "No," she finally said. "No, I'm not. I love you and that outweighs any other feelings I have."

"That's how I feel, too. I love you so much, I could never be ashamed of you."

Marianne threw herself into her father's arms and they embraced. It was a warm, solid hug, as solid as their love.

"Well," John said, ruffling his daughter's hair, "I certainly feel better. Maybe I could take you out to dinner and we could celebrate."

That seemed like a wonderful idea at first, but then Marianne realized that there was something more important she had to do.

"There's something I'd rather we do."

"What's that? You name it."

"Could we go back and talk to Mom?"

"You mean tell her the good news?" he said slowly.

Marianne nodded. "Not just tell her the news, but maybe you could talk to her, too," she suggested.

Now he was genuinely puzzled. "About what?"

"Dad," Marianne began, knowing he wouldn't like what she was going to say, "if Mom sees that we've made up, maybe you two could get closer, too."

He groaned. "Oh, honey, not again. You know a reconciliation with me is not in your mother's plans."

"But wouldn't *you* like it?"

Her father couldn't meet her longing gaze. "It doesn't matter what I want."

"I knew it. You would like to try it again. Why don't you talk to her."

"Honestly, there's no point."

"But before we had our fight, you said you were going to give it a shot. You never did," Marianne reminded him.

John's mind flashed back to the last time he had let his daughter persuade him to see Pat. It was a good thing his daughter didn't know what a fiasco that had turned out to be—white roses, an open screen door, and Pat's words: "I never should have married John."

But were those her real feelings? Perhaps she'd just said that for Dave's benefit. He hadn't had a discussion with his wife about their situation for so long, maybe he should give it one more try. It would be worth it if there was any hope at all. He looked down at Marianne's expectant face. "All right, honey, let's go see your mother."

Pat couldn't have been more surprised if her daughter had walked in the house with Santa Claus. Curled up in front of the television in her dressing gown, she was having a cup of tea when she heard the front door open. There were Marianne and John, walking into the hallway. Marianne seemed radiant; obviously, she and her father had made up. For his part, John looked uncomfortable but happy, and despite the problems she'd had with both her daughter and her husband, Pat was glad they had resolved their differences. Marianne's depression had been hard on everyone.

"Hello, Pat," John said tentatively as he came into the living room.

She swung her feet off the couch and sat up. "Hello, you two." She smiled. "It's good to see you both . . . together."

"Do you mean that?" John asked, hope in his voice.

"Yes, I do," she answered sincerely.

"Mom," Marianne broke in, "I was over at Dad's tonight and we got a lot of things straightened out. It made me realize I've been pretty hard on you, too, and I wanted you to know that I'm sorry. Can you forgive me for the way I've been acting?"

Pat rose to her feet and enveloped her daughter in a hug. "Was there ever any doubt?"

After a second or two, Marianne broke away and began speaking a bit nervously. "If you had asked me a week ago if I could make up with Dad, I would have said no way. But I have, and now I hope you two might be ready to speak to each other, too."

"Sweetheart, your father and I have been speaking lately," Pat said, flustered. "We've had several conversations about you since you started seeming so troubled."

"That's not exactly what I meant," Marianne said gently, "but I think this is my cue to butt out. You talk to her, Dad. Good luck," she whispered as she walked toward the front door. "Mom, I'm going out for a while. I want to see if Darrell is at the union."

"Fine," Pat said absently, not even noting that her daughter seemed to have rejoined the mainstream of life. Instead, her eyes were on her husband, and she was suddenly very conscious of being in her robe.

"Pat," John began as soon as Marianne left, "I still think we have a lot of unfinished business."

"Do you?" she asked with surprise. "Now that you and Marianne have patched up your differences, I hope things will get back to normal. But I think we have very little to talk about."

He ran his hand through his hair nervously. "Normal to me, Pat, would mean coming back to you."

She stared at her husband in disbelief. "You've got to be kidding. What in the world would lead you to think that we have a future together?"

"Marianne has forgiven me. I was hoping you could, too."

"John, it's hardly the same thing. I can't forget your affair with Barbara Weaver."

"Don't you think you're being a little too harsh?" he asked, grabbing her arm as she started to turn away.

Pat shook him off. "No, I do not. Why, I'm willing to bet you didn't even tell Marianne the whole truth during your little heart-to-heart tonight."

"What do you mean?" he asked, avoiding her eyes. But in truth, he had a pretty good idea where she was heading.

"I suppose you told Marianne all about your affair with Barbara."

"Yes."

"No doubt you said I was being secretive, and so you turned to Barbara for comfort."

"That's exactly what happened," John said a bit defiantly. "You can't deny it."

Pat looked at the floor. "Did you happen to mention that when I suspected something was going on, you lied to me. And, worse than that, you told Barbara I was giving you a divorce when we had never even talked about it?"

John hung his head and didn't say a word.

"I didn't think so," Pat commented bitterly. "Before Barbara left, we had a long talk. She said she didn't want to be involved with a married man, and the only reason she ever continued the affair was because she assumed she was going to be the next Mrs. John Randolph. She believed you, and you took advantage of her. That's the sort of behavior I can't forgive."

John walked over to the mantel and studied the pictures of his daughter. "Are you going to tell her?"

"Of course not," she replied in an exasperated tone. "Why would I want to devastate the poor girl all over again? She's found her way back to you and that's fine. Just don't expect me to do the same."

John turned and looked at his wife of so many years. In many ways, she was just as beautiful as she'd been the day he married her. She had the same elegant bearing and patrician features. If anything, the years had added a character to her face that made her more than just another pretty woman. Much more, he thought.

"Patsy," he said, using a nickname that dated back to the very first days of their courtship, "isn't there anything I can do or say to change your mind? We had so much together, and I know there could still be years of happiness ahead of us."

"Please," she implored, not wanting to hear him beg.

"I love you, Pat." It took every bit of courage he had to summon the words, but he made himself say it.

For a moment Pat's resolve almost weakened. To see John Randolph, the sophisticated attorney, standing in front of her a broken man was almost more than she could bear. Yet, when she analyzed her feelings for him, she realized that love was no longer among them. There was sympathy, some anger, even friendship, but not love. "I'm sorry," she said slowly, "but I think we've finally come to the end of our road."

There was one more question he had to ask, even though he dreaded it with every fiber of his being. Nonetheless, he'd never rest until he knew the answer. "Are you sorry you married me, Pat?"

She averted her eyes. This was something she had thought a great deal about in recent days. They'd had so many wonderful moments together and, of course, two beautiful children. But when she balanced all of that against the bad times, she was simply not sure which came out ahead. She could try to sugarcoat the truth, she supposed, but she knew in her heart he was waiting for an honest answer. "I can't say for sure, but, yes, sometimes I do think it might have been better if we'd never married."

So, those words he'd overheard her saying to Dave that night were not just spoken in anger

—they were the truth. He walked over to his wife and kissed her lightly on the forehead. "Good-bye, Pat," he said, looking deeply into her eyes. "I'm sorry."

Without another word, he turned and walked out the front door, feeling as though he was leaving behind everything in the world he held dear.

Chapter Eleven
Risky Business

Beatrice was sitting with Sally in the large, country kitchen going over her granddaughter's reading homework. The kitchen was one of the most charming rooms in the house, with gleaming copper pots hanging on the walls and blue and white Dutch tiles that added a cheerful note to the room.

Sally furrowed her brow as she sounded out a word. "The elephant gave the clown a ride on his back. Everyone laughed to see the funny sight." She took a breath when she came to the end of the sentence and turned to her grandmother. "How was that?" she asked.

Beatrice gave her shoulder a little squeeze. "Wonderful." Then she breathed a heavy sigh. "It's just too bad Alice isn't here to help you with your reading. Wouldn't it be nice if she could see how well you're doing?"

"She hears me sometimes," the little girl said, puzzled.

"Yes, sometimes," Beatrice said, pouring more milk in Sally's cup and adding a chocolate chip cookie to her plate. "Don't you think she should be here all the time to listen to you instead of working late? That's what real mommies do."

Sally sipped her milk thoughtfully. "Yes, it would be nice. Really nice."

"Your mother can't be here all the time, but that doesn't mean she loves you any less," Ray said, striding into the kitchen.

"Ray," Beatrice gasped, almost jumping out of her chair, "how did you get in here?"

"The side door was open. And a lucky thing it was, I see." He gave his mother a disgusted look.

Sally pushed away from the table and threw herself into her uncle's arms. "Can we go out for ice cream? You promised we could the last time you were here."

"You must be like that elephant you were reading about: you never forget," he teased. "Tell you what, you go out and watch some TV for a while and then we'll go. I want to talk to your grandmother for a few minutes."

"Okay," Sally agreed happily, running out toward the den. Meanwhile, Beatrice began busying herself, clearing away the food and dishes.

"Mother, why don't you put that down? I think we should have a talk," Ray said sternly.

"I'm real busy. You know how I hate a dirty kitchen."

"The work will wait," he said, physically removing some silverware from her grasp and leading her toward a chair. "Now, would you like to explain that little conversation I overheard?"

"I didn't raise you to eavesdrop."

"I didn't want to interrupt Sally's reading. Then you started in."

"I don't know what you're talking about," she said sullenly.

"Really? Well, it sounded to me like you were trying to undermine Alice's position and make Sally think she wasn't a very good mother."

"She's not a good mother."

Ray tried to keep his temper in check. "That is just your opinion, and there are many of us who think she is doing a great job of raising Sally."

"And you're one of them?"

"I certainly am."

"What do you know?" Beatrice burst out. "You're not here all day."

"Neither is Sally. She's in school."

"All I know is, I never would have treated my dear Jenny this way. Of course, that may be because she was my real daughter, my own flesh and blood."

Whatever civility Ray had managed to hold on to was lost. How dare she say something so insulting? "Jenny may have been your real daughter, as you so delicately put it, Mother, but she couldn't stand you."

"Ray!" Beatrice cried.

"I won't let you rewrite history. Jenny ran away and left us because she couldn't stand your meddling and interference. It was always, 'Wear this dress, Jenny. Date that boy. Don't date someone unless I approve.' You even read her diary and listened in on her phone calls. No wonder she couldn't wait to get away from you."

Beatrice slumped in her chair. It was so easy to pretend, now, that she and Jenny had had a wonderful relationship, but even she could not deny that what Ray was saying was closer to the truth.

"Mother," he said, more gently now, "either you are going to have to accept the way that Alice is raising Sally, or you are going to have to leave this house. If Alice is too nice to tell you that, I will."

"I don't want to move away from Sally," she said, dabbing her eyes.

"Then are you prepared to stop meddling?"

Beatrice nodded.

"Do you promise to stop interfering in Alice and Sally's relationship?"

She was cornered and she knew it. Ray would be watching her closely from now on, and she did so love Sally. It was worth any sacrifice to be near her, even if it meant going against her principles. "I promise."

Ray sighed. "I hope I can believe that."

Now it was Beatrice's turn to ask some questions. "You're planning to marry Alice, aren't you?"

He looked uneasy. "Mother, my divorce from Olive hasn't even gone through yet."

"That's why you came back, isn't it?" she insisted. "So you could be near Alice."

"So I could be near all of you," he stressed.

Beatrice let a mirthless little laugh. "I'm no fool, Ray. If it had just been Sally and me, you wouldn't have moved back here."

"All right, so I'm interested in Alice. What's wrong with that?"

"I'm not saying anything's wrong with it, but I'm warning you Ray, she isn't over Steve."

"Mother, Steve's dead."

"That doesn't mean a thing. Alice's heart still belongs to him. She may date you, she may even marry you, but you're always going to have the memory of that man to contend with."

Ray tried not to show his uneasiness at his mother's words. No matter how much he had tried to deny those very same thoughts, he knew that every time he was with Alice he was battling Steve's memory. How could he fight a ghost?

At many moments during the day—and at night —Alice wished that Steve was still with her. Now, facing Vic, she particularly felt in need of his strength. She had just confronted Vic with the evidence of his grossly inflated overbid for the City Hall renovation, and he was trying to tell her that it was not the bid he had made. She didn't know whether to believe him or not.

"Honest," he said for the second time, "I can't understand this."

"Well, I didn't want to tell you about it over the phone while you were out of town. I really thought we should talk about this face-to-face."

Vic looked down once more at the piece of paper he held in his hand. The bid was still $450,000, and it was in his own handwriting. But he was sure—no, positive—that he had written $150,000. He looked up at her anxiously. "You do believe me, don't you? This is not the bid I handed in."

Alice searched his face. He did not appear to be lying, but was she a good enough judge of character to really tell the truth?

Then she had an idea: she would see what Vic's response was to some of the other things that had been bothering her. "Well, let's talk about something else for a moment. I'd like to know why you haven't gotten back to me on that long memo I wrote you concerning the direction I think the company should take. I specifically asked for your input, and while I know you've been busy," she said, a bit apologetically, "I thought I would have heard something from you by now."

Once again, Vic's face was a study in confusion. "I don't know what memo you're talking about."

"I gave it to you weeks ago. I put it right on your desk," she argued.

"I do remember you saying you were going to write one. I never saw it though."

She didn't say a word, but disbelief was etched on her face.

"Look, it's obvious you don't think I'm telling the truth, but I am," he affirmed.

"I'm not saying that," she protested weakly.

"Fine, let's just go to my office and see if we can find that memo. We'll look through my files if we have to, and I'll prove to you that it's not there."

"Vic, this is silly. I can just give you another copy of it."

"No, I insist. I want you to feel you can trust me."

Reluctantly, she followed him across the hall into his office. "This isn't going to prove anything."

Distracted, Vic started rummaging around through the papers on his desk. By nature, he was a very orderly man, and he went through one pile of material after another while Alice stood at the side of the room feeling embarrassed. Then something caught her eye. Sticking out of his "in" basket, there was a document that looked like her note. She went over to the basket, pulled the paper out and examined it. Sure enough, it was her memo. Moreover, it sported a few coffee stains, making it look as though someone had read it quite thoroughly. Silently she handed it to him.

"I don't believe this," he said, flipping through the pages.

"It looks rather well read," she said coldly.

"Someone is out to get me. That's the only explanation for this."

Alice ignored his words. "If you didn't care for my comments, you could have just told me."

He threw a pile of papers down in disgust. "I swear to you, I'd never seen this document until just now, and I did not write that overbid."

Now Alice was even more confused. She had always trusted Vic, but in the face of the evidence before her, it appeared that he was a liar. On the other hand, he was defending himself almost too ardently. Could it just be an act?"

"Let me think about this, will you?" She rubbed her eyes wearily. "This is all very confusing, and I need some time to straighten it out in my mind."

"Certainly," he replied, trying to gain control of himself. He watched as she left his office and closed the door silently behind her.

Vic shakily sat down in his chair. Someone was definitely out to get him, and he had a pretty good idea of who it was. Right now, though, Willis held all the cards, and there was no way to prove that he was behind the dirty tricks. It would take some thinking, but Vic vowed that he'd find a way to reveal the truth.

Willis was standing at the file cabinet, pretending to look for some papers. He watched with interest as a dejected Alice walked back to her office. *Smart boy,* he thought. *You orchestrated that whole thing to perfection.* He'd known that today would be Vic's first day back in the office after a vacation and several business trips. Obviously, it would also be the morning Alice would go to him looking for some answers.

So, Willis had placed Alice's memo in Vic's box late the previous night. He thought the stains he'd added were a nice effect. Although he hadn't been sure that Alice would see the memo, from the look on her face, his plan had worked out just the way he hoped. He had to smile as he imagined the expression Vic must have had on his face when that piece of paper turned up.

Vic would probably be on to him at this point, Willis figured, but the man had no proof. None at all. He knew he would have to play things a little closer to the vest now, but at least the seeds of distrust had been planted in Alice's mind.

He chuckled wickedly. One of the secretaries looked up at him questioningly, so he turned his laugh into a cough and moved quickly toward his office. He sat down at his desk, but before he could get settled, Carol burst in waving a letter in her hand.

"What," she cried angrily, "is this all about?"

"Hey, calm down. I won't know until you show me what it is."

She threw the letter at him. "It's from Lowell Pendleton."

Willis leaned back in his chair with a smile on his face. "Oh, yeah? What does it say?"

"It says that Mr. Pendleton will hire me as the architect on the Washington project if I work up some sample drawings."

"Great!"

"Are you out of your mind? Robert is supposed to be the architect on this project and you know it."

He shrugged. "Pendleton must have changed his mind."

"I'm sure he didn't change it on his own. He would never have even heard of me without your interference," she accused.

"Guilty as charged," Willis said with a smile. "I just gave him a call—actually several calls—and talked you up."

Carol sank down into the chair across the desk from Willis. She was as upset as she could ever remember being. "Look, I don't know what you were thinking of, but there's no way I could handle that project. I don't have the experience. Surely you remember my problems with the shopping center."

"How could I forget," he replied grimly.

"Well, what do you think would happen on a project that's five times as large?"

"Look, we would call in some help on the financial part, someone's who's an expert on estimating costs."

"Robert is an expert on estimating costs."

Willis slapped his hand down on the desk. "How clear do I have to make this? I want you in place on that project. Robert is Vic's man."

"Robert is the man who can do the job," she said, near tears. "Don't you understand? If I take this job, it will be a disaster. It could ruin my name in the business."

"You're underestimating yourself, Carol. Look, the design work you've done for us has been spectacular," he flattered her. "The other things can be worked out."

She shook her head. "I don't think so."

When he saw that his words weren't having the desired effect, he came around his desk to where she was sitting and started massaging her neck. "Come on, sunshine, do this for me. It could be a real feather in both of our caps."

Carol began to melt. Maybe she could do what he was asking. After all, she knew she was a very talented architect. Just as she was about to throw caution to the wind and agree to Willis's request, she suddenly had a flashback of walking into her bank and taking out enough money to cover the overruns on the shopping center project. That had been a draining experience both emotionally and financially. If anything went wrong on this retirement village, Willis would probably expect her to do the same thing. But this time, it might be hundreds of thousands of dollars.

She jumped out of her chair. "I'm sorry," she said, "but I'm saving us both a lot of heartache by saying no. There's no way I'll be the architect on the Pendleton project."

Before he could use his considerable powers of persuasion on her, she hurried out the door, almost bumping into Sharlene on her way out. "Sorry," she said as the other woman moved away from the door so she could pass.

Forgetting the files in her hand that she had come to deliver, Sharlene went back to her own desk to consider what she had just heard. Carol, the architect for the Pendleton retirement village? How could that be?

Idly, Sharlene bent a silver paper clip back and forth in her hands. Her brother was getting very bold, there was no doubt about that. She was almost sure that he was responsible for Alice's not getting copies of Vic's correspondence. She would type the letters, make a carbon for Alice and deliver them. Several times, however, she had seen Willis coming out of Alice's office with what looked like the carbons in his hand. She had wondered if she should say something to Alice, but it always seemed silly. Why would Willis take carbons when he could ask for his own? Now she wondered if something much more serious was going on. After all, Willis had a reason for everything he did.

Her thoughts were interrupted by the buzz of the intercom. It was Alice asking if she could come into her office. She said she'd be right there, but the summons surprised her. She and Alice didn't do all that much work together, and it was unusual for Alice to have a special project for her. She hoped she hadn't done anything wrong. As soon as she stepped into Alice's office, however, she could see how depressed Alice looked.

"Hi. What's up?" she asked.

"Have a seat, Sharlene. I need to talk to you about a few things."

Sharlene looked around the office. When she had first seen it, it had been a masculine enclave, with lots of heavy wood and dark leather. Slowly, Alice was brightening it up, replacing woods with lacquers, adding prints by French Impressionists.

Alice followed Sharlene's glance. "Do you like what I'm doing with it?"

"Yes. It's comfortable, but it also has a lot of presence."

"At first, I didn't want to touch anything. It seemed like an insult to change things around. But little by little, I've started adding touches of my own. I hope Steve would approve."

"I'm sure he would," Sharlene said loyally.

Alice looked at the silver-framed picture of her husband that had a place of honor on her desk. "I certainly wish he were here now. I could use his help."

"What's wrong?" Sharlene asked with concern.

Sighing, Alice quickly outlined some of the conversation that had gone on between herself and Vic. "He said that after he wrote out the bid for the City Hall project, he left it on your desk for you to type and mail. Do you remember doing that?"

Sharlene shrugged, a bit confused. "I type so many bids for so many different people."

"Think, Sharlene, this is important."

She searched her memory. "I do seem to remember Vic handing me a bid and saying that this project would be a special one for you."

"That's the one," Alice said eagerly. "Do you recall how much the bid was for?"

Sharlene shook her head. "Frankly, Alice, I don't even remember typing it. I just put it in the stack of work I had for that day, and I assume it got done eventually."

Alice was clearly disappointed. "I see."

"I'm terribly sorry," Sharlene said.

"It's not your fault. There was no reason why you should remember it. I was just hoping you might corroborate Vic's story."

"I wish I could," Sharlene said sincerely. "I can tell you that I've always found Vic to be an honest man and a wonderful person to work for. I can't believe he would do anything to undermine you."

"That's what I thought, but what other explanation is there? The bid clearly said $450,000 in what even Vic admits is his handwriting. And that report he claims he never got was right on his desk—with coffee stains on it, no less."

"It does look pretty bad," Sharlene admitted.

"He seems to think someone is out to get him, but I don't buy that. Would you?"

Light bulbs suddenly went off in Sharlene's head. How could she have been so stupid? Now it all made sense. Willis could easily have changed the bid and stolen the memo, replacing it when he knew it would make Vic look the worst. This would explain Willis having Alice's carbons as well. It would be another way to make it look as though Vic wasn't keeping Alice informed. Even Willis's conversation with Carol fit into the picture. He wanted the Pendleton project for himself; there was no doubt of that. Willis was out for Vic's job.

"Sharlene," Alice asked with concern in her voice, "are you all right? You're suddenly very pale."

"No, no, it just got a little warm in here, don't you think?" she lied. Sharlene knew she should share her suspicions with Alice immediately, but she had no proof. And if she was honest with herself, there was a more pressing reason: she was afraid of how Willis would react if she told anyone that he was to blame for Vic's troubles.

There was only one thing she could do, even if it was just a meager effort to soothe her guilty conscience. "I'm sure Vic is telling the truth," she said, more forcefully than before. "You should trust him."

"You really believe that, don't you?"

"I certainly do. If Vic says someone is out to get him, that's probably the truth, as hard as it is to believe."

"I'll keep that in mind. And look, I don't have

to tell you that whatever we've said can't leave this office."

"Of course not." Sharlene rose shakily to her feet. "I think I'd better get going. I have to relieve the new girl at the reception desk in about five minutes."

"Go ahead. You're sure you're all right?" Alice repeated.

"Yes, I'm fine, honest. I'll see you later." She practically ran out of the office and into the ladies' room, where a couch was provided for employees who didn't feel well.

Kicking off her shoes, she lay down on the couch, her eyes closed and her hand pressed against her forehead. *What should I do?* she wondered. Alice had been so good to her. How could she betray her? The same was true of Vic. That man had been a good employer and a better friend.

And yet, she knew that crossing her brother was like stepping on a rattlesnake. He was unpredictable . . . and dangerous.

Chapter Twelve
Trouble for Sharlene

"Wear this one!" Sally called from the closet. Sharlene had to laugh. She could barely see the little girl herself, much less the dress she was talking about.

A small hand with a fist full of a pink print material was sticking out of the closet, so Sharlene walked across the bedroom and plucked the dress off its hanger. Sally came out right behind it.

"You like this one?" she asked doubtfully. She held it up to herself and looked in the mirror. "I'm not sure that pink is my color."

"I think it's beautiful," Sally sighed.

"It's almost new, that's for sure. I've barely worn it. Well, let me try it on again." Quickly, she took off the blouse and sweater she had worn to the office and pulled the pink dress over her head. Maybe it was because she had lost a few pounds, or perhaps she had just never noticed how well the pale print went with her dark hair and eyes. In any case, the dress seemed just right for the big night Russ had promised her.

"When I grow up, I'm going to have a beautiful dress and date a handsome man like Uncle Russ," Sally assured her from the bed where she now sat.

"I have no doubt about that," Sharlene said, removing the dress carefully. She then slipped into her terry-cloth robe. "You're going to be the prettiest girl in ten counties."

Sally beamed. "Thanks, Aunt Sharlene."

"Pumpkin, you're going to have to excuse me now. I'm going to take a bath and get ready."

"Where are you going?"

"I don't know. He just said to wear my prettiest dress and get all gussied up because we were going to have a very special night."

"What does 'gussied up' mean?" Sally asked, frowning.

"It means making yourself beautiful."

"Which your Aunt Sharlene is not going to have time to do unless we leave her alone," Alice said, coming into the room.

"I was helping," Sally protested.

"I'm sure you were, but it's time we start getting you ready for bed."

"Can't I wait up for Uncle Russ?"

"If you go in right now and put on your pajamas. Now scoot."

Sally jumped off the bed and headed for her bedroom. "I hope she wasn't bothering you too much."

"Not at all. She just added to the fun of getting ready."

Alice patted her sister-in-law's shoulder. "That's nice of you to say."

Sharlene looked into Alice's sweet, open face and felt terrible. It had only been a little more than a day since she'd figured out what Willis was up to, but she still hadn't decided what she would do about her suspicions.

Even though Sharlene didn't have any proof of her brother's wrongdoing, she knew she was doing Alice a disservice by not confiding in her. Her guilt had made her want to avoid Alice, a feat that was a little difficult to accomplish when they lived in the same house and worked in the same office.

Sharlene pointed to the shampoo and soap she had picked up from her dresser. "Alice, you're going to have to excuse me," she said apologetically.

"Certainly. You get ready and hopefully Sally and I will have your Prince Charming waiting for you when you come downstairs."

She took a little longer than usual getting ready, but seeing the effect she had on Russ made it all worthwhile. He smiled proudly as she came down Alice's curved staircase.

"You look lovely, Sharlene," Russ said sincerely, and Alice nodded in agreement.

Even the often insecure Sharlene knew that this was true. It was one of those evenings when everything just seemed to come together. Her haircut was now a little longer, and she'd styled it into a sophisticated wave. The strapless pink dress hugged her figure, and her new sandals made her legs look long and sexy. She finally felt like the assured, together woman others assumed her to be.

After they said their good-byes, Russ and Sharlene headed for his sporty convertible and drove out toward the bay.

"Isn't it about time to tell me where we're going?" she asked after a while.

He turned to smile at her in the dark. "Not a chance. Everything tonight is going to be surprise. Just one surprise after another for my lady."

"And the first is the restaurant we're going to?"

"Absolutely."

He drove and drove until she wondered if they were going to wind up in Chicago. She was not far wrong. They were on the Chicago side of the bay when Russ pulled into a secluded driveway that led to a small parking lot.

"This is a restaurant?" she asked, puzzled. "It looks like someone's house."

He went around to the passenger side of the car, and helped her out. "Actually, at one time it was." They walked up the gravel road to the steps of an imposing Victorian house that had a discreet sign that said: REGENT'S HOUSE RESTAURANT.

When they entered, Sharlene was charmed to see the house had been beautifully restored to its original glory, and all the furnishings matched the turn-of-the-century time period in which the house was built. The hostess led them to one of the quaint wooden tables. Gaslights flickered on the walls and the table was set with heavy silver and damask linen.

"Russ, what a marvelous place. How did you ever find it?"

"Even a busy doctor hears about wonderful new restaurants."

Music gently wafted into the dining room from the garden just behind the French doors. "That reminds me, before we order, may I have this dance?" He led her out to the garden where a trio in tuxedos played a Viennese waltz. Chinese lanterns lit the patio, where several other couples swayed in time to the music.

It was a beautiful evening, and they lingered over their supper and danced between courses. Finally, however, it was time to leave.

"Russ," she said after they had been driving along for several miles, "this isn't the way back to Bay City."

"Smart girl," he replied, giving her a little pat on the knee.

"Well, if we're not going home, where *are* we going?"

Russ pulled into a shady, isolated spot where they had an excellent view of the bay. "Right here."

"Pretty romantic. Is this where you take all your girlfriends?"

"Hardly. Just the ones I want to do this to." With that, he pulled her closer, and gave her a long, lingering kiss.

She looked deeply into his eyes. "You take my breath away."

"That's all right. I'm a doctor; I know how to

resuscitate you." Before Sharlene could even smile, he kissed her again.

They sat quietly for a few moments, looking at the moon shimmering on the lake. Then Russ began talking. "Sharlene, no one thinks I'm impetuous, but sometimes I am."

"What do you mean?"

"Well, if most men were going to do what I plan to tonight they would have taken some precautions, asked opinions, gotten advice."

She wasn't sure what he was talking about. "What opinions and advice?"

"Some men might have asked you your opinion about marriage, for one thing."

The color drained from her face, but he just continued talking.

"Another guy might have wanted to make sure he knew the answer before he asked this question. Sharlene, will you marry me?"

"Are you serious?"

Ignoring her question, he said, "Another guy might have wanted your advice about a ring." He pulled a small, black leather box out of his pocket and opened it up. Sitting in a nest of velvet was a perfect diamond ring.

Sharlene looked up at him with tears in her eyes. "I love it."

"You do? Here, let me put it on you." Carefully, he slipped the ring on the third finger of her left hand. It winked in the moonlight.

"I take it by accepting my ring, you are also accepting my proposal?" he asked with a smile on his face.

"Yes, darling, I am." They kissed passionately, but when they broke away, the tears in Sharlene's eyes were now slipping down her cheeks.

"Those are tears of joy, I hope."

"Russ," she said, now gripped with an unnameable dread, "are you sure about this?"

He laughed. "Yes, very sure."

"You don't know all that much about me," she reminded him. There was a little catch in her voice.

"I know I love you."

"I haven't wanted to talk about my past," she said, dabbing her eyes with her handkerchief, "because it's been pretty sad."

He took her in his arms. "I know we've both had more than our share of sadness in this life. That's why I want to spend the rest of my life making you happy. I hope you feel the same way about me, darling."

"I do, Russ," she said firmly. She was about to add something else, but she faltered, unable to summon the courage. Instead she murmured, "It's just that our backgrounds are so different."

"So, you come from a farm in Chadwell, and I've always lived in a medium-sized city. Big deal."

"It's not just that, Russ. You know all of us Frames were dirt poor. You and Pat and Alice had wonderful childhoods."

"We did, but so what? Besides, no one was more in love than Alice and Steve, a Frame and a Matthews. I rest my case."

"But, Russ—"

"No more 'but Russes.' You love me, don't you?"

"Yes," she replied quickly.

"Then, that's all that matters."

"If you say so," Sharlene said with a nervous smile.

"Now, on to more important matters. Like, when's the wedding?"

The small knot of fear inside her, which had loosened slightly, tightened itself back into a hard ball. "I can't think about that right now. This whole thing's been quite a shock, you know."

"I guess I can understand that," Russ said agreeably, "but name me a season, a time of year when you'd like to be married."

"Christmas," she said. It was the first thing that popped into her mind.

"Christmas?" he replied, disappointed. "It's barely summer now. How about autumn?"

"I . . . I don't know, Russ."

"How about Labor Day weekend, if we could arrange it, that is."

A loud no slipped from her lips. It reverberated in the quiet night air.

He looked at her with dismay. "Honey, you do want to marry me, don't you?"

"Of course I do," she said in a flat tone.

"You don't seem very enthusiastic about the idea. Is something wrong? Is it the ring? We could always exchange it."

Sharlene was overcome with guilt. She threw herself into Russ's arms and gave him several quick kisses. "The ring is gorgeous, darling, it's just . . ." she hesitated.

"Just what?"

"I don't think I'm worthy of you." That, anyway, wasn't a lie.

He looked at her tenderly. "Oh, my dearest Sharlene, is that what this is all about? You're really that worried about our backgrounds?"

Sharlene nodded silently.

"You are the love of my life. Nothing will ever come between us." He took her in his firm grasp and held her tightly.

But there are things that could come between us, she thought, looking at the stars. *Things you don't know about me*. And then there was Willis. Who knew what trouble he could cause? *Oh, Russ, I'm so afraid.*

Despite Russ's protests, Sharlene decided she wanted to keep their engagement a secret for a while. Naturally, he had been eager to tell his sisters and father the good news, but Sharlene had persuaded him that their engagement would be all the dearer to her if she could keep it just between the two of them for now. She wore her engagement ring on a silver chain around her neck, only putting it on when she knew she would be alone with Russ.

Sharlene realized this charade was silly and that everyone would find out sooner or later. But somehow, she felt the longer she could keep the news from leaking out, the safer her love would be.

Work was now becoming a hassle, as well. There had been no new treachery against Vic, at least

none that she knew about, but she doubted if her
brother had stopped his underhanded tricks. At the
office, she tried to avoid him but that was not
always easy. One day, her heart sank when he
ordered her into his office.

"Hi, big sister," he said in a chummy tone.
"Have a seat."

She perched herself carefully on one of his
chairs. She did not dare get too comfortable.

"So what's new?" he asked amiably. "It seems
like I never see you anymore."

Sharlene pasted a smile on her face. "Willis,
how can you say that? I sit right outside your office
every day."

He continued to stand, moving a little closer to
her. "But that's not the same as really seeing each
other. Why, when we were kids, we were practically inseparable."

Her mind flashed back to those long-ago days in
Oklahoma. They were inseparable all right. He was
usually tagging after her, and if she stepped out of
line, he'd tattle, ensuring that she got a spanking.
"I remember," she answered curtly.

"You know," he added, gazing out the window,
"I think families should stay together."

"Hmmm," she muttered noncommittally.

"Now if you came to me asking for a favor, you
know I wouldn't turn you down."

Right, she thought, *as long as you could turn it to
your own advantage.*

"So naturally," he continued, "when I ask you
for a favor, I'd appreciate some consideration."

"Cut the fancy talk," she finally said, her patience running out. "You want something from me. What is it?"

Willis tried to look hurt. "Is that any way to talk to your brother?"

"That's right. You're my brother and we go way back, so don't try to pull the dedicated relation act on me. I know you too well for that," Sharlene said bluntly.

"Fine," Willis agreed, wiping the smile from his face. "We'll do it your way. Here's what I want: from now on send any calls from Lowell Pendleton directly to me, even if he asks for Vic."

"You've got to be kidding."

His expression turned to ice. "I don't kid."

Before she could stop herself, she blurted out, "I know what's going on around here, Willis, and I don't want any part of it."

"What do you think is going on?" he asked in a tight voice.

Suddenly, she knew she had gone too far. "Nothing."

"I don't believe that. Come on, tell me."

She was starting to get angry. How dare he try to take over this company for himself. He had no right to do such dishonest things, and to hurt people she cared for. The more she thought about it, with Willis standing threateningly over her, the madder she became. Finally, her fury exploded. "I know your rotten little plan to take over this company. Stealing memos, falsifying bids, I know all about it, Willis."

"And *how* do you know?" he asked, so quietly she almost couldn't hear him.

She looked at him defiantly. "I'm not as dumb as you think."

Willis's lip curled into a half smile. "No, you're dumber. Telling me all this was hardly the brightest idea in the world."

"Why not? Someone has to stand up to you and maybe I'm the only one who knows you well enough to do it."

Now he laughed in his sister's face and her bravado quickly left her. "You're going to tangle with me? Think back to when we were kids. Did you ever win a fight?"

"There's always a first time," she said, her voice shaking.

"Yeah? Well, this won't be it. You see, I'm not the only one with secrets. You have a few, too, don't you?"

Sharlene's eyes grew huge with fear. "What are you talking about?"

"Don't you know? Well, let's see, where should I start. First off, I wonder why you didn't tell me about your engagement."

Sharlene's hand flew involuntarily to her neck.

"That's right, you wear your ring on a chain instead of on your finger, where any happy bride-to-be would have it."

"How did you know?" she whispered.

Willis folded his hands across his chest. "We both have a very talkative young niece. Sally told me all about the pretty, sparkling ring you have on a chain. It made me stop and think."

"Russ and I aren't ready to announce our engagement yet," Sharlene said defensively. "What's the big deal?"

"Somehow, I don't think this is Russ's idea. I'll bet it's you who doesn't want to set a wedding date."

"That's silly. Why shouldn't I want to set a date?"

Willis shrugged. "Maybe there are some things you're afraid Dr. Matthews will find out about his new bride."

She began shaking a little, but she tried to hide it. "You've got it all wrong."

"Let's be honest with each other, shall we, sis? I need a favor from you. Are you going to do it?"

"Give you Vic's calls from Pendleton? No way."

"Then I won't be able to do a favor for you."

"What favor?"

"Keep your little secret about San Diego."

All the color drained from Sharlene's face. *My God, he knows!* "What about San Diego?" she managed to ask.

He shot her a contemptuous smile. "Why, I know all about it and if you don't do as I ask, Russ and the rest of Bay City will know about it, too. So, you'll help me out, won't you, Sharlene?"

Her mind was whirling. She saw all her pretty, hopeful plans for the future crumbling before her. The secret she had tried to keep buried for so long was out. Willis knew.

"So what's your decision?" he needled. "With me or against me? It's time to decide."

Soaps & Serials™